Twisted Perfection

ALSO BY ABBI GLINES

Twisted Perfection

Abbi Glines

SIMON AND SCHUSTER

First published in Great Britain in 2013 by Simon & Schuster UK Ltd
A CBS COMPANY

First published in the USA in 2013 by Atria Paperbacks,
an imprint of Simon & Schuster, Inc.

1 3 5 7 9 10 8 6 4 2

Simon & Schuster UK Ltd
1st Floor
222 Gray's Inn Road
London
WC1X 8HB

Simon & Schuster Australia, Sydney
Simon & Schuster India, New Delhi

A CIP catalogue copy for this book
is available from the British Library.

ISBN: 978-1-4711-2041-1
Ebook ISBN: 978-1-4711-2037-4

Printed and bound by CPI Group (UK) Ltd, Croydon, CR0 4YY

www.simonandschuster.co.uk
www.simonandschuster.com.au

Abbi loves to hear from her readers. You can connect with her on
Facebook: Abbi Glines (Official Author Page)
Twitter: @abbiglines
Website: www.abbiglines.com

To Autumn Hull. Listening to me while I'm lost in my creative process isn't easy. It can be annoying. Having someone you know you can call and complain to is priceless. Thank you, Autumn.

Acknowledgments

Keith, my husband, who tolerated the dirty house, lack of clean clothes, and my mood swings while I wrote this book (and all my other books).

My three precious kiddos, who ate a lot of corn dogs, pizza, and Frosted Flakes because I was locked away writing. I promise, I cooked them many good, hot meals once I finished.

Colleen Hoover, Tina Reber, Autumn Hull, Liz Reinhardt, for reading and critiquing *Twisted Perfection*. Thanks for your help, ladies!

To the coolest agent to ever grace the literary world, Jane Dystel. I adore her. It is that simple. And a shout-out to Lauren Abramo, my foreign rights agent, who is doing an amazing job at getting my books published worldwide. She rocks.

Most important, God. He gave me the ability and creativity to write. The fact I get to do what I love every day is a gift that only He can give.

Three years ago

Della

You are my sunshine, my only sunshine. You make me happy when skies are gray.

Don't stop singing now, Momma. Not now. I'm sorry I left. I just wanted to live a little. I'm not scared like you are. I need you to sing. Please sing for me. Don't do this. Don't go to him. He wasn't real. Don't you see? He was never real. He died sixteen years ago.

I should have told someone about you. This is all my fault. You needed help and I didn't get you any. Maybe I was scared after all . . . scared that they would take you away.

"Della, sweetie, give me your hands. I need to clean them off. Look at me, Della. Come back to me. She's gone but you're gonna be okay. We need to clean you up. They've taken her body and it's time to leave this house, for good. No coming back. Please, Della, look at me. Say something."

I blinked away the memories and stared up at Braden, my best friend. She was cleaning the blood from my hands with a wet washcloth, and tears were streaming down her face. I

1

should have gotten up and cleaned this all off myself, but I couldn't. I needed her to do it for me.

⋙

I always knew that one day this would happen. Maybe not the exact way it was happening. I hadn't ever imagined my mom dead. Most days when I let my daydreams turn to this moment, I'd feel guilty. It wouldn't stop me from thinking about it, though. The guilt wasn't enough to keep me from imagining my freedom.

⋙

I had always thought someone would realize my mother wasn't all there. They would figure out that I wasn't some strange child who wanted to stay inside all day and refused to come out into the real world. I wanted them to . . . but then, I didn't. Because getting my freedom would mean losing my mom. As crazy as I knew she was, she needed me. I couldn't let them take her away. She had just been so scared . . . of everything.

Della

When Braden gave me her old car and told me to get out and see the world, neither of us thought about the fact that I didn't know how to fill it up with gas. I had had my driver's license for only three months. And I'd actually had a car to drive for only five hours. Pumping gas wasn't something I needed to know until now.

I reached into my purse and pulled out my phone. I'd call Braden and see if she could talk me through this. She was on her honeymoon and I hated to interrupt her, though. When she'd shoved her keys into my hand earlier today and told me that she wanted me to "Go explore. Find your life, Della," I'd been so caught up in the awesomeness of her gesture that I didn't think to ask anything else. I'd simply hugged her and watched as she ran off with her new husband, Kent Fredrick, and crawled into the back of a limo.

The fact that I couldn't pump gas had never crossed my mind. Until now. My tank was so empty I'd coasted into this small service station in some beach town in the middle of nowhere. Laughing at myself, I listened as Braden's voice said,

"I'm not available. If you want to reach me I suggest you hang up and text me." Her voice mail. She was probably on a plane. I was going to have to figure this one out all on my own.

I stepped out of the small, faded red Honda Civic. Luckily I'd pulled up to the gas pump on the correct side. There was the little door I knew the nozzle went in. I had seen Braden do this before. I could do this. Maybe.

My first problem was that I couldn't figure out how to open this magical little door. It was there. I could see it, but it had no handle. I stared at it a moment, then glanced around to see if there was anyone near me who didn't look scary. I needed some help. It had taken two solid years of counseling to get me to speak to strangers. Now I did it often. Braden really had more to do with that than the psychologist I'd been forced to see weekly. Braden had pushed me out into the world and taught me how to live.

I had the quote "The only thing we have to fear is fear itself," by Franklin D. Roosevelt, taped to my bathroom mirror. I read it daily, or at least I had been, for the past three years. I silently quoted that in my head, and my body relaxed. I wasn't scared. I wasn't my mother. I was Della Sloane and I was on a road trip to find myself.

"You okay? Need some help?" A deep, smooth drawl startled me and I jerked my head around to see a guy smiling at me from the other side of the gas pump. His dark brown eyes appeared to twinkle with laughter as he stared back at me. I didn't have much experience with guys, but I had enough to know that even when they were gorgeous, like this one, it didn't make them a good person. I had lost my virginity to a smooth-talking Southern boy with a smile that made panties drop all over the place. It had been the worst experience of my

4

life. But this guy might be helpful. He wasn't offering sex. He was offering to help me. At least I thought he was.

"I can't . . . I, um . . . See, I've never . . ." God, I couldn't even say it. How did a nineteen-year-old girl explain that she didn't know how to pump gas? Laughter slowly bubbled up in my chest, and I covered my mouth. He was going to think I was insane. I swallowed my laughter the best I could and smiled up at him. "I don't know how to pump gas."

The guy's elegant dark eyebrows shot up, and he studied me a moment. I guess he was trying to decide if this was true or not. If he only knew. There was so much I didn't have a clue about. Braden had been trying to educate me in the ways of the world but she was married now and it was time I figured things out without her as my crutch.

"How old are you?" he asked, and I noticed his eyes slowly scan my body. I didn't look like a teenager. My body had been fully developed by the time I was sixteen. I could tell he was trying to figure this one out. Youth would be the only explanation he could come up with for the fact that I couldn't pump gas.

"I'm nineteen, but I've not been driving that long and this is the first time I've had to pump gas." I sighed and then chuckled. This sounded ridiculous, even to me. "I know it sounds hard to believe, but honestly, I need some help. If you could just get me started, I can do this." I looked back at his big, fancy truck. It was all shiny and black. It fit him and his tall, muscular body, olive complexion, and dark hair. He was one of those sexy, beautiful, dangerous ones. I could tell that by the smirk on his face.

When he stepped around the corner, I realized that he was much taller than I had originally thought. But then, I was only five foot five. The snug fit of his jeans and dark brown leather

5

work boots did really good things to his legs. I realized a little too late that I was staring and jerked my gaze up to meet his amused one. He had a really nice smile. All-white, perfect teeth framed by a face that looked like it hadn't seen a razor in a few days. His scruffy appearance didn't fit with his expensive truck.

"You need to pop this little door open first," he said, tapping his knuckle on it. The way his lips curled seductively around his words fascinated me to the point that I worried I'd missed further instructions. I was just about to ask when he walked around me and opened the driver's door to the car. He bent over, giving me an unobstructed view of his jeans tightening over a delicious firm backside. I really liked this view.

The magical door that had baffled me sprang open and startled me. I squealed and spun around to see it now standing open. "Oh!" I exclaimed in excitement. "How did you do that?"

His large, warm body came up behind me and I could smell grass and something richer . . . maybe leather. The alluring scents engulfed me. Seeing as I wasn't one to miss an opportunity (I'd missed too many of those in my life), I moved back slightly, just enough so my back was touching his chest.

He didn't move away from me invading his personal space. Instead, he'd lowered his head to talk into my ear. His voice was low and rumbled deliciously. "I pressed the gas door button. It's in your car, just under your dash."

"Oh" was all I could think of to say as a response.

A low chuckle in his chest vibrated against my shoulders. "You want me to show you how to actually put the gas in the car now?"

Yes, that would be nice, but I really enjoyed standing like

6

this, too. I managed a nod, thankful that his body didn't move. Maybe he liked the physical contact just as much as I did. This was really a bad idea. I should move. Guys like him didn't treat women well. Why did they have to smell and look so wonderful?

"You're gonna have to let me get around you, sweetheart." His warm breath heated up the hair covering my sensitive ear. I tried not to shiver as I managed a nod and hurriedly moved away to press my back against the car so he could get past.

Our chests brushed lightly as he maneuvered around me, holding my eyes with his penetrating gaze. The warm chocolate brown with gold flecks in them didn't seem so amused anymore.

I swallowed hard and glanced down. Once he was safely away from my body, I decided it was time to watch him pump my gas. I needed to remember this was a lesson. One I'd desperately needed.

"You have to pay first. You got a card or are you paying cash?" His voice was back to normal. No more sexy low whispers in my ear.

Money. I'd forgotten about the money. I nodded, leaned into the car to dig in my purse, and pulled out my wallet. I grabbed my debit card and stood back up to hand it to him. His eyes were on *my* bottom this time. The thought of him checking out my backside made me smile. A little too brightly.

"Here," I said, handing it to him as his eyes ran back up my body. He took the card and winked at me. He knew I'd caught him looking and he was enjoying it. This one was a player, the kind a smart girl ran from. I wasn't that smart though. I'd given my virginity to a guy just like him. It had been in the guy's best friend's apartment. Little did I know his "best friend"

7

was actually a girl who was madly in love with him. That had not ended well.

He was scrutinizing my debit card. "Della. I like that name. It fits you. It's sexy and mysterious."

At that moment, I realized I didn't know his name. "Thank you, but now you're one up on me. I don't know your name."

He smirked. "Woods."

Woods. That was unique. I'd never heard the name Woods before.

"I like it. Fits you," I replied.

He looked like he was going to say something else, but then his smile turned serious and he held up the card. "Lesson number one is how to pay for it."

I watched and listened carefully as he explained each step of working a gas pump. It was hard not to get sidetracked by the commanding way he carried himself. Sadness swept over me when he placed the pump back on the machine and tore off my little slip of a receipt. I didn't want this moment to be over, but I had a road trip to get back to. After all this time, I needed to concentrate on finding myself. I couldn't stop now, just because a guy caught my attention at a service station. That would be silly.

"Thank you so much. Next stop won't be so hard," I said, taking my card and receipt and clumsily trying to shove them into the pocket of my shorts.

"Any time. You vacationing here?" he asked.

"No. Just driving through. I'm on a road trip to nowhere and everywhere."

Woods's eyebrows narrowed and he studied me a moment. "Really? That's interesting. Do you know your final destination?"

I didn't have a clue. I shrugged. "Nope. I guess when I find it I'll know it."

8

We stood there a moment in silence. I started to move, when Woods's hand reached over and touched my arm. "Have dinner with me before you get back on the road? It'll be dark in an hour. Won't you be stopping soon anyway to get a place to spend the night?"

He had a point. This was a nice little town—very classy and coastal. It seemed to be a safe option. I really wasn't worrying about safe, though. I was finally living. I was throwing caution to the wind. I stared up at the dark stranger in front of me. He wasn't safe. Not in the least.

"Dinner sounds nice. Then maybe you can point me to the best place to get a room for tonight."

Woods

I kept the little red car in my rearview mirror. I was having Della follow me just out of town to a Mexican restaurant that had really good food. And there was a better chance I wouldn't run into anyone I knew.

Tonight was about taking a break from the stress that my life had become. My dad was pushing me more and more to prove myself. I wasn't sure what the hell else he wanted from me. No, that wasn't true. I knew his plans for me. He expected me to get married. Not to someone of my choosing, though. He had already chosen who he wanted me to marry—Angelina Greystone. All my life, Dad had planned on having the Kerrington name linked with the Greystone name. He'd had his eye on the prize. Every year we'd spend a week in Hawaii with the Greystones, and Dad always encouraged me to get to know Angelina. For us to spend time together. Hell, they'd pushed us together so much at such a young age that we'd ended up having sex at fifteen. I'd thought I was her first until I'd actually slept with a virgin and realized Angelina had been lying. I might have been a virgin that year, but she sure hadn't been. It had jaded my view of the pretty blonde. The older and more glamorous she became, the more I ran like hell to stay away from her. She had claws and she wanted them deep in me. I knew the day would come when I'd cave just to make my dad happy, but I was putting it off as long as I could. Or I had been until Angelina had moved south. She was now taking up residence in her parents' beach house, and my dad was forcing her on me constantly.

I needed to step back from all the shit that came with being a Kerrington and hopefully enjoy this hot little number who had the body of a sex goddess and the face of an angel.

She seemed skittish at first, but then some wild, carefree girl emerged, and I wasn't one to turn away sexy invitations. That body and those big blue eyes had been all the hinting I needed. Better yet, this one wasn't sticking around. I'd get a naughty distraction who wouldn't come with the high-maintenance syndrome later. She'd just drive away.

The memory of that ass of hers stuck up in the air in those tiny shorts that barely covered it up had me shifting in my seat to adjust my excitement. Della Sloane was just what I needed tonight.

I pulled into the gravel parking lot of El Mexicano and parked on the far side of the building so that someone driving by wouldn't notice my truck. No interruptions tonight. I was getting laid. The hot no-strings-attached kind of laid.

I stepped out of the truck and watched as Della got out of her car. She wasn't wearing a bra under that black halter top. Those tits of hers held the fabric up like one big tease. Damn, this was gonna be a good night. I was more than positive she wanted this, too. She'd all but pressed her ass against my dick after I opened her gas tank. This one knew what she was doing and she did it well.

"Good choice. I love Mexican," she said, smiling at me.

I watched her hips sway invitingly as she walked my way. I was about ready to forgo the meal and head straight to the hotel room. Her dark hair fell just below her shoulders in soft, natural curls. I was also more than positive those long, dark eyelashes were the courtesy of good genes and not out of a package. I'd seen my share of false eyelashes on females and these looked real.

"I'm glad," I replied, stepping forward and placing my hand on the small of her back to lead her inside.

⚸

Once the food was ordered, Della took a sip of her margarita and smiled at me. "So, Woods, what do you do for a living?"

I wasn't answering that truthfully. I didn't like to give a woman too much info into my life unless I planned on keeping her around. "I work in management."

Della didn't frown or look perturbed that I'd blown off her question. She kept smiling and sipping the sweet yellow drink.

"Obviously you aren't ready for the hard questions. I'm good with that. How about you tell me what you love to do."

"Golf, when I get time, and taking really hot females out to eat Mexican food," I replied with a smirk.

Della threw her head back and laughed. She was so free of inhibitions. She wasn't trying to impress me. It was refreshing. Her eyes twinkled when she looked back at me. "What's your biggest fear?"

Whoa. Weird turn of questioning. "I don't think I have any fears," I replied.

"Sure you do. Everyone does," she said before licking at the salt around her glass.

Did she have fears? It sure didn't look like it. "Becoming

12

my dad," I said before I could stop myself. That was too much for her to know. More than I admitted to anyone.

A faraway expression came over her face as she stared past my shoulder. "That's odd. My fear is that I'll become my mom."

Her big blue eyes blinked rapidly and a smile came back on her face. Wherever she'd gone mentally, she was back. Thinking about her mom wasn't something she wanted to do and I understood that.

"What do you love to do?" I asked her, wanting to change the subject back to something light.

"Dance in the rain, meet new people, laugh, watch old eighties movies, and I like to sing," she replied, then smiled at me before taking another sip. At this rate she was going to get hammered if I didn't watch her closely.

⚭

Two margaritas later and she was pressing her chest against my arms while laughing at all my jokes. I was cutting her off now because she was just the right kind of tipsy. I didn't want her completely drunk.

"You ready to go find that hotel room of yours and let me get the bed nice and warm for you?" I asked, grinning down at her and slipping my hand between her legs. She froze at first, then slowly eased them open so that I could move my hand up high enough to feel the dampness against her panties. She wanted me just as much as I wanted her. That was confirmation enough. I ran the tip of my finger up the wet crotch of her panties and she trembled against me.

She moved against my hand and closed her eyes while her mouth fell slightly open with a blissful look. *Damn*, she was responsive.

"Is this what you want?" I whispered in her ear as I slipped a finger inside her panties and felt the hot, moist temptation with no barrier.

"Yes," she breathed. "But only if you promise you'll make me come."

Fuck. I snatched my hand out of her panties and grabbed my wallet. I slapped a hundred-dollar bill on the table. We didn't have time to wait on a ticket.

I wanted exactly what she was promising. As for making her come, I'd make sure she passed out from the number of orgasms I intended to give her. Never throw a Kerrington a challenge like that one. We will go above and beyond.

She wasn't going to be able to drive her car like this. I'd figure out how to get it back to her later. I didn't have time to think about that right now. I opened my truck door and put her inside with more force than I'd intended. Her big blue eyes went round with surprise and I stopped to catch my breath and think this through. Maybe I shouldn't do this. Was that nervous flash in her eyes really innocence? Her body was telling me one thing but those eyes were saying something else.

She pulled her bottom lip into her mouth and bit down. I wanted to taste that mouth.

I didn't walk around to my side. I'd get to that later. I crawled up in the truck and closed the door behind me before grabbing each side of her head and tilting it just right. My mouth covered hers and I let her taste slowly sink into me. Each small moan from her lips pounded through my veins. The fullness of her bottom lip as it moved against my mouth with inexperienced hunger was driving me mad.

I forced myself to pull back and look down at her hooded eyes. "Are you sure you want this? Because if you're not, we need to stop now." We'd never see each other again. I needed to know she wasn't the innocent that I kept sensing in her touch. I wasn't against one-night stands if the girl knew what she was in for. I needed her to be clear on this.

"I," she said, then paused and swallowed hard. That wasn't the answer I was looking for. I started to move back away from her, but she reached out and grabbed my shirt. "No, wait. I want this. I need it. Please, don't stop."

I still wasn't sure. She didn't sound positive. "Is this your first one-night stand?" I asked, thinking that may be the reason behind the way she was acting.

She shook her head no, and a small, sad smile touched her lips. "No. The last one I had was bad. Really bad. I want you to make me forget it. I want to know what it feels like to just do it for pleasure. Nothing else. Just make me feel good."

She wasn't a virgin. That was good. A bad one-nighter would make anyone unsure about doing it again. I could make her forget it. "I'll make it feel real good, sweetheart," I assured her. Then I reached down and took the bottom of her little excuse for a shirt and pulled it over her head. She wasn't wearing a bra. I'd known that, but seeing her bared to me was still breathtaking.

"Oh," she squealed, and fell back on her elbows, which only pushed her breasts out farther toward me. I was a tit man. There was no doubt about it, and I was pretty damn sure I'd died and gone to heaven.

"These babies are fucking incredible," I swore before lowering my mouth to pull one of her round, candy-red nipples into my mouth.

"Oh, yes," she cried. I smiled to myself. Normally I didn't like the vocal ones, but this one wasn't practiced. She was real.

Every cry out of her mouth sounded like she meant it. I filled my hands with both of her breasts and spent equal time teasing and sucking. I was pretty damn sure I could do this all night and not get bored.

"Ah! Please, I need you inside me. I wanna come," Della begged.

I wanted her to come, too, but if she didn't stop making those naughty demands, I was going to come first in my damn jeans.

I reached for the waist of her shorts and jerked them and her panties down at the same time. I threw them to the floor before spreading open her legs with both my hands. She was waxed. *Fuck yes*. The sexy scent of her arousal met my nose and I growled in appreciation. I needed to taste this. I wanted that orgasm she was begging for to happen in my mouth first.

I touched the smooth skin and ran a finger down the center. Della bucked wildly against the leather seat. "I'm gonna kiss this," I warned before pressing my lips to the swollen clit sticking out, in need of attention.

"Ohmygod," she moaned, and both her hands grabbed the back of my head. I couldn't keep from smiling.

I licked gently at first and then began tasting more earnestly. She really was delicious. I'd tasted many women, but this one was sweet. I pressed the tip of my nose against her clit as I slid my tongue inside her. Both her hands fisted in my hair as she cried out my name. I loved hearing her say it. Probably more than I should have for a one-night stand I'd never see again.

The reminder that I wouldn't see her again made me a little frantic. I needed more. I began licking her with more intensity. Until that first orgasm erupted on my tongue and she

16

screamed my name over and over. It was the first time I'd ever come close to losing it in my jeans since high school.

I pressed one more kiss to her tender flesh before sitting back and unbuttoning my jeans. I should wait until I got her to a hotel room, but I needed to get the edge off first. If I was only getting one night with this girl, then I was going to enjoy her over and over again. This first fuck would get me stable enough so that I could drive to the nearest hotel.

I jerked open my glove compartment and pulled out one of the condoms I kept in there. I tore the wrapper off and slid it down over my dick before looking at her. She was watching me closely. Her pink tongue came out and wet her lips. I groaned and pulled one of her legs up over my shoulder so I could move in between her legs comfortably.

"What if someone sees us?" she asked, still breathless from her very vocal reaction to her orgasm.

I laughed. She was just now thinking about that. "These windows are tinted, it's dark, and there is no light around us. We're also pretty damn high up in this thing. No one's going to see us."

She gave me a sexy smile and let her hands fall back over her head, causing those tits to jiggle. This wasn't gonna last long. I was too damn close.

I pressed the head of my cock to her opening and slowly began pushing in. She was tight. Too fucking tight. *God, no, please don't let her be a virgin.* Girls that looked like her were not virgins at her age. She was meant to be fucked. "You're tight," I bit out.

She nodded and moaned, opening her legs wider. "I'm not a virgin," she reminded me.

Right. Why was it I kept wanting to slow down and ease

17

her into this? She was hot and ready. The worry that she was innocent was screwing with my head. I slammed into her and we both cried out. She was incredibly fucking tight but she hadn't been lying; there was no barrier. She wasn't a virgin; she just had a pussy from heaven. Damn, this was incredible.

I slid back out of her and she reached up and grabbed the handle on the door, bracing herself for me to pound back into her. "Hard . . . please . . . again," she panted.

I didn't have to be told twice.

I managed to hit it even harder this time, and those tits of hers bounced beautifully. I was pretty sure I'd never get over them. I was gonna come. This was too much.

I slipped my hand down between us and ran my finger over her clit several times until she was panting and pleading. "You like that? Such a naughty girl. Asking me to fuck you harder," I whispered against her ear as I used the wetness pouring out of her to lubricate her swollen clit.

"Ohgod, Woods. Ohgod, I'm gonna come again," she cried, and I pulled her nipple into my mouth and sucked while playing with her clit.

She exploded beneath my touch, and I grabbed the back of the seat and the dashboard for support as I slammed into her only two times before I followed her into release.

Della

I slowly peeled my eyes open and stared up at the ceiling. The hotel room was silent. I was alone. I was also relieved. I wasn't sure how I could face Woods after last night. I was a lot of things, but a whore wasn't one of them. Thinking back to last night's events, I felt very much like a whore. I wasn't sure what had possessed me . . . unless it was the tequila. Maybe my courage to take what I wanted had come from a little too much to drink, but I hadn't been drunk. I'd known exactly what I was doing.

Woods was hot, dripping with charisma, and did I mention hot? And I didn't even know his last name.

I covered my face with both my hands and started to laugh. I'd had wild monkey sex with a man I'd just met. How crazy was that? At least he'd used a condom each time we'd done it: in the truck, in the shower, against the table, and then finally in the bed. After which I'd promptly passed out. I'd wanted to know what good sex was. Now I knew what earth-shattering sex was. Mission accomplished. One thing was for sure. I'd never forget Woods. This was a trip to experience life, and with Woods I had managed to experience one of the finer things in life.

Stretching, I stood up and glanced around the room for

my clothes. Wait . . . my car. I needed my car. My luggage was in my . . . Uh, my luggage was sitting at the foot of the bed. What? I had left it in my car. I pulled the sheet from the bed and wrapped it around me. Then I walked over to the window and pushed back the curtain. It didn't take me but a minute to find Braden's red car parked out front. Woods had gone and gotten it for me and brought my luggage inside.

My heart warmed at his thoughtfulness. If I was going to have sex with a random stranger, at least I'd chosen one who didn't leave a girl completely stranded.

Present day

I sat in the office of Jeffery Odom, my current boss, waiting on him. He'd texted me this morning and asked me to come into work early and meet him here. I wasn't sure what was wrong. A couple of weeks ago, he had started flirting with me and then it had become something more. I had worried this would be a problem. I was a waitress in his bar. I was also only here for a short time.

On this trip to find myself I was having to stop and get jobs until I had enough for another couple of weeks of traveling the road. I liked Dallas. It was fun. Jeffery was sexy and older. He made me feel special. At least when he was in town.

In the beginning he'd been around only once a week, but after a few flirty moments between us, he started showing up more and more. Mostly at closing time. He would wait in his car and text me to meet him outside. This secret romance was starting to get annoying, though. It wasn't as if I was taking it seriously. I needed another five hundred in tips and I was back on the road. Next stop, Las Vegas.

The door to his office finally opened, and the frown on his face alerted me that this wasn't a fun visit. I might be heading for Vegas sooner than I thought.

"I'm sorry I called you in here so early, Della," he said, walking to the other side of his desk and sitting down. This was all very proper and cold considering I'd been taking a shower with him only three nights ago before finally giving in and having sex with him.

I didn't respond to him. I wasn't sure what to say.

Jeffery ran a hand through his hair. "I think it's best if you moved on earlier rather than later. This thing with us has gotten too serious and we both know it isn't going to last."

Okay. So he got what he wanted and now he wasn't even going to let me make my last five hundred before I headed out. He knew I was close to leaving. *Bastard*.

"Fine," I replied, and stood up. I didn't need this. I could stop short of Vegas and get another job.

"Della," he said, standing up with me. "I'm sorry."

I just laughed. He was sorry. Not nearly as sorry as I was. I thought we'd become friends.

I headed for the door and realized this was another one of those experiences I was on the road to find. I'd been used. I was living life. It wasn't such a hit to my ego if I thought of it like that.

Before I could reach the door it swung open, and a tall, elegant redhead stepped inside with an angry snarl . . . directed at me.

"Is this her? Is this your whore? Figures, she looks like a fucking slut. Did you find this one at one of those disgusting strip joints you go to? She looks like a stripper. God, Jeff, how low could you stoop?"

21

I listened to her words, but I wasn't sure I understood what she was saying. I was confused. The only thing I was positive of was that this woman hated me. Something fierce. I wasn't sure why, but she did.

"That's enough, Frances. I've fired her like you requested. Let her leave. This is between you and me," Jeffery said to the angry redhead. He glanced my way and I could see the apology in his eyes.

I looked back at her and the temper that was boiling out of control as she glared at him. "You fired her and that makes it okay?" She swung her hateful gaze back to me. "Do you even care that you were fucking the father of my unborn child? Does it bother you at all that he's not only married but going to be a daddy soon?"

Wait . . . *what?* Did she just say married?

I stared at her and realized that this wasn't a sick joke. Then I turned my head and looked at Jeffery. The truth was there on his face. He was married. He had made me an adulterer. Oh. Shit.

"You're married?" My question came out as more of a roar than a question.

He nodded and his shoulders sagged as if he was defeated.

I took a step toward him and stopped. If I got any closer I was going to kill him with my bare hands.

"You sorry sonofabitch! Why would you . . . how could you . . . you have a *wife* and she is *pregnant*! I can't believe you did this. I'm *so stupid*. So incredibly stupid! All the sneaking around wasn't because you didn't want the other employees to know. It was because of her." I pointed at his wife. "I hope you burn in hell," I swore, then spun around and headed for the door. Before I could open it and get the hell out of there,

22

I stopped. There was someone else I needed to say something to. I looked back at the redhead. Her anger had faded. Her face was now streaked with tears.

"I'm sorry. If I'd known he was married I wouldn't have gone near him. I swear it." Then I stormed out the door and slammed it behind me.

When I stepped back into the bar, my eyes met Tripp's. He shook his head and sighed. "I was afraid you'd hooked up with him, but I wasn't sure. I didn't want to say anything in case I was wrong and ended up offending you. I'm guessing you didn't know he was married."

I felt dirty and wrong. I walked over and sat down on the stool across from him. "I had no idea. And now I feel awful. I wanted this road trip, but now I just want to go home."

Tripp was the Thursday-through-Sunday bartender. He was tall and lanky and had short brown hair. He also had a little bit of a privileged look about him. It was hard to explain, but something about Tripp didn't fit in here. He seemed as out of place as I felt. We had spent many late nights talking while shutting down the bar. I didn't know much about Tripp, but he'd become my friend here.

"You said you wanted to see the world. To live," he said, reminding me of my words.

I shrugged. "Not so much anymore."

Tripp glanced back at the door and then reached into his pocket and pulled out his phone. "I tell you what. Don't go home just yet. Give yourself some time to heal from this and then hit the road again. Spend some time in a small town and take things slow."

The way he explained it sounded nice, but I wasn't sure I was up for that, either.

"I'm going to call my cousin. He has some pull in the coastal town I grew up in. It's small and it's a really nice place. Nothing like Dallas. My cousin can hook you up with a job and you can decide when you're ready to hit the road again. He has friends in high places." Tripp winked.

Before I could protest or come up with a reason why this was a bad idea, Tripp was dialing his cousin's number.

"Hey, Jace. . . . Yeah, I know it's been a while. Life gets crazy. . . . No, you need to come to Dallas and tear yourself away from the girl your momma said you're so wrapped up in you can't see straight."

Tripp laughed, and I could see the happiness in his eyes. He loved the cousin he was talking to and it looked like he might miss him, too.

"Listen, I need a favor. I got a friend. She's had a hard go of things here and she needs somewhere to escape to. . . . No, I know you got a girl. I'm not asking you to take her in, idiot. She can stay at my place there. Someone might as well get some use out of it. Just talk to Kerrington. Have him give her a job. She just needs some downtime. . . .Yeah. She is. I'm positive he'll be pleased. . . . Awesome. Thanks, man. I'll call you back in a few. I'm gonna get her the info she needs and send her your way."

Tripp grinned as he slipped the phone back in his pocket. "It's all set up. You'll have a good-paying job and you can stay in my condo there free of charge. I've been needing to send someone over to check on it. With you there you can take care of things. It will help me out. Then the best bonus, you'll be living near one of the most beautiful beaches in the South. Go find yourself while in the sunshine, Della."

Woods

I paced in front of my desk. Every now and then I glanced down at the diamond ring sitting in the center of it. I knew what it meant. I also knew I wanted to throw it as far out into the damn ocean as I could. This was my dad's not-so-subtle hint.

I'd gone to him yesterday to ask him when I would get to move on from management and take my place as a vice president of Kerrington Country Club. This was his answer. I had to marry Angelina.

Fuck! Fuck! *Fuck!*

I didn't want to marry her. She would make me miserable. I'd finally given in last month and had sex with her again. She'd shown up at my house in nothing but a tiny red nightie, dropped to her knees, and sucked my dick. Between getting my cock sucked and the whiskey I'd been chugging, I'd fucked her several times that night. Problem was, the only way I'd managed to get off was by picturing the pretty blue eyes of Della Sloane looking up at me. Angelina's cries of pleasure turned me off. She was practiced in faking it. She didn't like sex. She used it.

I knew her type well. I wasn't interested.

I wasn't my father. I couldn't marry for money and con-

25

nections and then have a woman on the side. It always made me angry that my parents' screwed-up marriage didn't seem to affect them. It completely messed with my head.

If I was going to tie myself down to one woman and be faithful to her the rest of my life for the sake of my rightful place in the family business, I wasn't sure I wanted in. Fuck all this shit. My dad was always controlling me.

A knock on my door stopped my endless pacing and silent ranting. I grabbed the ring and shoved it into my pocket. I didn't need this getting out. And God help me if that was Angelina.

"Come in," I called out, and took a seat behind my desk.

Jace, my best friend since boarding school, opened the door and stepped into the room. "Hey, I thought you'd join us on the course for a round this morning but you never showed."

I needed to talk to someone about this, but I wasn't sure I was ready. Jace would tell me to leave town and let them figure this shit out on their own. He'd been rebelling against his father's wishes for years now. "I got busy" was my only response.

Jace nodded. "Yeah, I figured." He walked over and took a seat across from me. "I need to ask you for a favor."

That got my attention. Jace didn't ask me for favors often. I leaned back in my seat and waited. This had better not be about getting his girlfriend, Bethy, who was also one of my beer cart girls, off work early. We had a rush in the evenings and I needed her.

"I got a call from Tripp," he started. Tripp was his older cousin. He'd graduated a couple of years before us, but we'd had one awesome year in boarding school together before he left. I hadn't seen him since he packed up and left town five years ago.

"Really? How is he?" I asked curiously. I'd always liked Tripp. He hadn't wanted to bend to his parents' demands, either, so he just left. Never looked back.

Jace shrugged. "Good, I guess. He sounded happy. He's in Dallas now. I need to make it out there and see him. He didn't come to Boston this Christmas with the rest of the family. I don't expect he'll be coming around anytime soon. Uncle Robert isn't happy with him."

I didn't imagine Robert Newark was happy with his only son. He was supposed to inherit the prestigious Newark and Newark law firm located in Destin, Florida. His grandfather had built the firm from the ground up. But Tripp hadn't wanted to be a lawyer. He'd wanted to travel the world.

"Anyway, there's this friend of his. She got mixed up with their boss at the bar and come to find out he was married. She didn't know and she needs to get out of town and heal and shit. He asked if he could send her here. He said she's an excellent waitress. She's a hard worker and she's never late. He also said she's gorgeous and the men here would tip her well. He's letting her stay at his place since it sits empty all the time, but she needs a job."

I could always use good waitresses. "Of course. Just send her to me when she gets in town. We'll get her a uniform and put her to work."

Jace looked relieved. "Thanks. I hated to ask but he sounded worried about her. He's already called me twice today to talk about her and make sure I get everything ready for her arrival. I didn't want to let him down."

"I understand. I don't mind. And tell Tripp I said the next time he wants a favor to call me. I'd love to hear from him."

Jace hadn't been gone long when the door to my office opened and in walked Angelina. She tossed her long blond hair over her shoulder and smiled at me. It was that practiced seductive smile. It bored me. Her tongue darted out and she licked her lips while sauntering over to my desk.

"I've missed you. I haven't seen or heard from you since last week. I thought we'd had fun on the sixteenth hole."

I had agreed to take the last round of the day last week with Angelina. I knew it would get my dad off my case and satisfy her. What I hadn't expected was for her to rub against me and grope my dick the entire time. The last time she slid her hands down the front of my shorts and said she wanted to be fucked, I bent her over and placed both her hands against a tree, then screwed her from behind. That way I didn't have to see her fake expressions of pleasure. She was doing this to get me to marry her. Her daddy wanted this and she was doing what he wanted. Nothing more.

After I'd gotten my release, I'd ended the game and dodged her ever since.

"I've been busy," I replied coldly.

She didn't take the hint. Instead, she stepped between my legs and leaned over me, giving me a direct view down her shirt. She didn't have much in the way of tits. I wasn't sure what she was flashing me. If I married her, I was getting her a boob job.

"Too much work and not enough play," she cooed, dropping to her knees and rubbing her hand over my uninterested cock.

"I can take the edge off," she promised, and went to unfasten my pants. I had felt bad the last time I'd let this go too far. I was using her. Sure, she was using me, too, but it didn't mean I had to stoop that low. It was wrong. I didn't want her. If I did marry her, it would be because I was being forced to. There was no reason for me to keep this charade up. I needed some time to think about all this.

"Stop, Angelina. I have work to do. Not now." I resisted the urge to shove her away. That would be too cold.

"You can work and I can make it feel good. Show you what you can have the rest of your life."

We both knew that the moment I said "I do," sex between us would become a chore. She'd make up reasons why she couldn't, and office blow jobs would be a thing of the past.

"Don't take me for a fool, Angelina. I'm a smart man. I know what you're doing and I know why. The minute we're married this facade you're putting on will disappear."

Her eyes flashed with resentment. I was just being honest. It was time she was, too.

"Just because my daddy wants me to marry you doesn't mean that is the only reason I want to. I'm attracted to you. What woman isn't? The difference between other women and me is that I'm good enough for you. We complement each other. You can fight this and try like hell to hold on to your playboy ways, but I won't go anywhere. I want that ring I know your daddy bought on my finger and I want your last name. The sex could be incredible for us both if you'd just let it. I won't always be the whore you fantasize about. You should enjoy that part of it while you can."

She stood up and straightened her skirt. "You know where to find me when you're ready to admit this is perfect. You and me."

Della

I pulled over at the service station where I'd met Woods only four months ago. It had been the start to my journey. How ironic that the directions Tripp had given me led me right back here. I wasn't even sure Woods lived in this town. He'd taken me a town over to eat and find a hotel. Maybe he'd just been driving through that day, too. Or maybe I might see him again.

What if he's married?

No, I wasn't going to think that. I wasn't going to judge all men by Jeffery. That was unfair. Take Tripp, for example. He was nothing like Jeffery. He had given me the keys to his condo to stay in free of charge as long as I kept it clean. He'd also gotten me a job.

I glanced down at the paper in my hand. Tripp had given me Jace's phone number and told me to call him once I was settled in. He'd get me an appointment with Mr. Kerrington.

I got back out on the road and followed the last two turns before pulling up to a condo unit that faced the ocean. I glanced down to check the address Tripp had given me. Surely this wasn't his condo. This town was high-end and these condos had to all cost a fortune. How did Tripp own one?

The nagging suspicion that Tripp didn't belong working as

a bartender and driving a Harley-Davidson came back to me. He was something more than he was letting people in Dallas know.

I pulled my cell phone out of my purse and dialed Tripp's number. No answer.

I then dialed Jace's number. It rang three times and a girl answered.

"Hello," she drawled.

"Um, yes, I'm, uh, Della Sloane. A friend of—"

"Tripp's!" she squealed into the phone. "We've been expecting you. I'm so glad you made it safely. Are you settled into Tripp's apartment yet?"

I was pretty sure he had said Jace was a guy.

"Um, no, not exactly. I just arrived and this place is really nice. I'm afraid I'm at the wrong condo."

The girl laughed. "No, you're at the right place. I'm assuming you don't know that much about Tripp. Trust me, honey, he can afford that place and more. Oh, I'm Bethy, by the way. Jace's girlfriend. He's outside."

I liked her. She was superfriendly.

"If you're sure I'm at the right place, I'll go find his unit and unpack my bags. I need Jace to contact Mr. Kerrington about meeting me."

"Oh, there's no reason to call him. He told Jace to send you to him as soon as you're ready. He needs some new servers. Do you have a pen and paper handy? You need to jot down these directions."

⚽

This was quite possibly the nicest place I'd ever stayed. Tripp made it sound run-down, like he needed me to come stay here and fix things up. Someone obviously cleaned this place regularly. It was in pristine condition. I unpacked my bags and then went to stand out on the balcony overlooking the Gulf of Mexico. It was beautiful out here. Tripp had been right. This was an experience I needed. I could work and enjoy staying here in his condo. It would be the beach vacation I'd never gotten growing up. I'd always watched television and wondered if the sand was that white and the water was that blue.

It was.

Smiling, I sank down onto the lounge chair and stretched my legs out in front of me. This was nice. I pulled my phone out of my pocket and dialed Braden's number.

"It's about time! Where are you? Still in Dallas?" Braden's chipper voice made me miss home a little. Maybe I just missed her. It wasn't like I'd left a lot behind there. Except for people who would always whisper about me and wonder.

"Nope. Not in Dallas anymore. Turns out Jeffery is married."

I heard her sharp intake of air as she let that sink in. "Oh, no," she breathed. "Della, that's awful! I'm so sorry. Where are you now? Do you want me to come get you? You're doing okay, aren't you? Not having strange thoughts . . ." Her voice trailed off. I knew she hated to ask me that, but honestly, if Braden couldn't check on me that way, then who could? She knew it all, or most of it. No one knew all of it. I just couldn't share everything with the world. Some things were meant to be kept a secret.

"I'm fine. I'm actually back in Florida, staying in a condo that belongs to Tripp—he's the weekend bartender I told you about. Anyway, he hooked me up with a job in his hometown and gave me a place to stay. It's gulf front. I'm sitting on the balcony looking at the pretty white beach now."

"Ooooooh! That sounds wonderful. Lucky you! I would love to visit the gulf again sometime. And this Tripp guy sounds really nice. Maybe once you've gotten the traveling bug again you could head back to Dallas and thank him," she teased.

"Tripp is just a friend. Not happening. I mean, I'll thank him, but I'll be sending a card and some money or something via the mail."

"You're right. I pushed you to start dating and look what happened. This is your chance to live life. No reason to get attached to one guy. You have the world to explore."

"That's right. And I intend to do that right after I enjoy the sunshine and sand for a little while."

"What's the new job like?"

"I'm not sure yet. I need to go meet the boss. He's expecting me. It's at a country club, so that should be a fun experience. Much different from the bar," I told her.

"Very. Go get that job, then call me and tell me all about it. I can't wait."

We said our good-byes and ended the call. Braden was always my way of touching base. Remembering things. Everything I had been through and everything I had overcome.

The night I met Braden had changed my life. The only person I'd ever known before then was my mom. She wouldn't let me answer the door to receive packages or our groceries. I'd had to hide in my closet and be quiet until the person at the door was gone. Braden had been as fascinated with me as I was with her. She'd asked me questions that I hadn't been able to answer for a long time. I couldn't tell anyone what was wrong with my mom. Even as a kid I understood that.

Shaking away memories I didn't want to think about right now, I stood up and headed for the bedroom I'd claimed as mine. There were two bedrooms, and one had a king-size canopy bed and a fabulous hot tub. I took that room. I pulled out my newest skirt—a short pink chevron print—and a white sleeveless knit top I'd bought to go with it. After brushing my hair and applying some makeup, I slipped into a pair of backless pink heels and headed for the door. I had a job to claim.

Woods

I hated management. This was how my father was wearing me down. He knew I hated this part of the job and he also knew I didn't deserve to be doing it. He was using this torture to get me to marry Angelina. And it was working, dammit.

I shoved open the kitchen doors to deal with the latest drama and found my head server, Jimmy, with his hands on his hips, glaring down at the newest server, Jackie or Frankie or something I couldn't remember. She was crossing her arms over her chest and glaring right back at Jimmy.

"What the fuck is going on? I need you out there serving guests and I hear you in here fighting as I walk by. Someone want to explain, or do I just fire all your sorry asses?" I demanded in a tone I knew couldn't be heard outside the kitchen walls.

"I can tell you what's wrong. Her. You hired a lazy one. She takes a smoke break every ten minutes, and if I have to serve another one of her tables because she's left the order sitting there for more than five minutes, I'm gonna go apeshit on her ass. You hear me? Either she goes or I go."

I wasn't firing Jimmy. He ran the kitchen for me. He was also a favorite of the female members. They had no idea he preferred the male members. It was a secret we kept so that he got the nice big tips.

I turned my attention to the new girl. "I thought I made it very clear when I hired you that there were no smoke breaks. Jimmy says when anyone takes a break. He is the boss in here."

The girl let out a sigh and then jerked her apron off and slung it on the ground. "I can't work with these kinds of slave conditions. A girl needs a break, and just because I'm not as fast as he is, he gets mad. Well, screw him. I'm out of here." She spun around and stalked out of the kitchen.

Good. I didn't have to fire her or deal with female tears. Only problem was that I needed another server. Now.

"Glad she's gone, but we need to call in backup," Jimmy said, stating the obvious.

"Try to manage until I can get someone in here to help." I headed out the door and was making my way to the office when the click of high heels alerted me that I was being followed. *Please, God, not Angelina now.* I wasn't in the mood. Unless she wanted to go serve customers, she needed to leave me the hell alone. I turned around to tell her so when the words froze on my tongue.

It wasn't Angelina. It was Della. She was even more mouthwatering than I remembered, and I remembered a lot. Almost every damn day I remembered her really well. Normally while I was in the shower.

Her dark hair looked longer, and it was pulled to one side and laid loosely over her shoulder. She was wearing a snug-fitting white top that didn't leave a lot to the imagination with that chest of hers. Then a short skirt and a pair of heels that made her tanned, slender legs look even sexier. What was she doing here?

"Woods?" she asked, and I raised my eyes from taking in every detail of her body to meet her surprised and confused gaze.

36

"Della," I replied. Did she not come here looking for me? Why did she seem so surprised?

"What are you doing here?" she asked as a pleased smile started to form on her lips. I'd never told her my last name. On purpose. I didn't want the one-night stand to turn into anything more. Although over the past four months I'd kicked myself for not giving her my number. I'd wondered where she was and if she was going to come back this way anytime soon. Now here she stood. In my club.

"My father owns the place," I replied, and watched her face. Her eyes went wide and she glanced around at her surroundings as if taking them in for the first time.

"Are you Mr. Kerrington?" she asked.

"Depends. My dad is also Mr. Kerrington. I typically go by Woods."

Della let out a soft laugh. "I can't believe this. I think I'm supposed to be meeting with you about a job. Tripp sent me."

Tripp. This was the girl? The one he was helping out? Shit! What had Jace said happened to her? She had gotten messed up with the boss or something. Hell, I couldn't remember. I hadn't paid that much attention.

"Yeah, that would be me," I replied. There were plenty of reasons why this was a really bad idea. I didn't need this kind of distraction. I had to find a way to deal with my dad and Angelina. Seeing Della every day was going to fuck with my head.

"I hope this is okay? I mean, he never said 'Woods.' He always referred to you as Kerrington." The nervous tone in her voice snapped me out of my internal battle.

"Uh, yeah, uh, just come on back to my office and you can fill out paperwork and we can discuss where you would fit best."

Far away from me. Far, far away. I needed to put her sexy

37

ass on another continent. But I was about to give her a job. Here at my club. So I could be tortured with the memory of our night of amazing, mind-blowing sex. *Ah, hell.*

I didn't wait for her to catch up to me and walk beside me. I was afraid I would be able to smell her and I'd have her pressed up against a wall with my hands all over her in minutes. Instead, I stalked ahead of her and didn't look back. I knew she was following me only by the click of her heels.

Once I finally got to my office door, I opened it and stood back so she could step inside. I held my breath until I was safely away from her.

"Woods, you seem really unhappy about this. I'm sorry. I didn't know. I didn't even know this was the town Tripp was sending me to. He gave me directions and sent me this way. I was desperate to leave, so I did. I can get a job somewhere else if this is weird for you."

The worried little frown scrunching up her nose made me crumble. I couldn't do this. I couldn't be hard or cold with her. I was going to give her the damn job, any job she wanted, and I was going to stay the hell away from her. Maybe I should propose to Angelina. That would keep me from making the mistake of hunting Della down every chance I got.

"I'm sorry. This is fine. I've just had some issues with employees and drama in the kitchen to deal with. You surprised me. But you have a job here if you want it. Just tell me what you're good at." *Other than fucking my brains out.*

Della sat up straight and my eyes drifted down to her tits. The outline of her pebbled-up nipples sent my already hardening cock to complete attention. Fuck, she was turned on. She was remembering, too.

"I've been working at a bar in Dallas as a waitress. That's

38

normally the kind of jobs I get. They're easy and the tips are good, so I don't have to stay around too long."

I nodded. That's right. She was traveling the world. She wasn't putting down roots in Rosemary. She didn't want a relationship. She wanted an adventure.

"You want a server job here? It's an easier crowd than a bar and I just lost a server right before you walked in."

I wasn't putting her far away from me. No, I was putting her right here under my damn nose. I was a fucking idiot.

"Thank you. That would be perfect. Do you need me to start right away since you just lost a server? I'm a quick learner," she assured me.

No, I needed her to go back to Tripp's condo and let me calm the fuck down.

A knock on the door interrupted me before I could respond and Jimmy stuck his head in. "It's getting out of control." His eyes found Della and he flashed her a smile. "Well, aren't you all kinds of sexy. Please tell me you're here for a job."

Della smiled at him brightly and nodded.

"Perfect. Can I have her?" Jimmy asked, opening the door wider.

I wanted to tell him no, that I wasn't done with her yet. I was still considering laying her over my desk and pushing that skirt up to see what she had on underneath.

"Sure. Go ahead and take her. She has experience so it shouldn't be hard to get her going."

Della stood up and smiled back at me one more time. "Thank you for this." Then she went to Jimmy, who closed the door behind them.

I laid my head back against the leather seat and let out a defeated sigh.

39

I needed to remember that Della would be leaving soon. She wasn't one to stick around. I couldn't lose everything I'd worked for because I wanted to be buried in her tight little pussy again. It was time I focused on Angelina. Maybe having that buffer between Della and me would keep me from making a mistake. Because Della Sloane could cause me to lose it all. Then she'd walk away.

As sweet as she tasted and as perfect as she felt, I couldn't let my desire for her change my life. Angelina would make my dad happy. I'd be vice president, and this management shit would be behind me. It was my only choice. It had to be.

Della

*D*on't touch that food, Della. It's your brother's. It's his favorite. You know that. Why do you always try and throw it away? Why, Della? Why would you do that to him? Be a good girl, Della. Sweet and good."

"But, Momma, it smells bad. It's old and there are flies—"

"SHUT UP! SHUT UP! Go to your room. We don't want you in here. All you do is complain. Go to your room. Go to your room."

"Momma, please just . . . Let's fix him a new plate. This one has gotten old. It's making the whole house smell bad."

"He wants you to leave it alone. He's coming to eat it. Just go to your room, Della. Go sing a pretty song. One we can all enjoy."

I didn't want to sing a song. I wanted to throw away the rotten food. I shook my head and started to protest, when she grabbed me around the neck and started shaking me.

"I told you to sing, Della. Leave your brother's food alone. It's his, damn you, girl. Such a selfish brat," she screamed in the high-pitched voice I knew to fear.

I pulled at her hands and fought for air. I couldn't breathe. She was going to choke me. A trickle of something wet touched my cheek and I looked up to see blood raining down on me. It

41

was her blood. It was my momma's blood. Looking down at my hands, I saw they were covered in blood. I turned to cry for help but there was no one there. I was alone. Always alone.

⋙

I sat straight up in bed as the scream ripped through my chest. Opening my eyes, I took in the unfamiliar surroundings. The large picture windows in front of me showed the early morning sunlight dancing across the ocean waves. I gripped the down comforter in my hands and took several deep breaths. I wasn't back in that house. I was safe. Everything was okay. My body trembled as I sat silently and watched the beauty that I had found myself immersed in.

I didn't know if my memories would eventually disappear or if one day they would consume me. Until then, I needed to live. Every time I thought about going home and giving up on this trip to find myself, I had my dreams to remind me of why I had to do this. My time was limited. Shoving back the covers, I made my way to the bathroom to take a shower. The sweat covering my body from the nightmare made my T-shirt cling to my skin. Every morning for the past three years I had woken up like this.

⋙

The end of day two at work and I'd not seen Woods since I walked out of his office. I was beginning to think he was avoiding me. Maybe that was best. He was my boss and I'd already had a taste of how badly dating your boss could go. I guess Woods was making sure we put the past behind us. Considering Woods had given me my first-ever orgasm that I hadn't had to work for made having to move on a little hard, but I could do it.

I was ready to enjoy life, not worry over or want things I

couldn't have. This was supposed to be a fun, carefree trip. It was time I started making it one. Jeffery had really put a hitch in my plans. He'd also taught me that men could be pigs. I needed to remember that.

An attractive brunette with a sincere smile stepped out of the fancy car parked beside mine. Her focus was on me. I paused as she closed her car door and walked toward me. She wasn't dressed like the female members our age that I'd seen while in the dining room. She was wearing a pair of faded, well-worn, skintight jeans that hung low on her hips and a tight Corona T-shirt. The red stiletto heels on her feet looked hard to walk in.

"You must be Della. You're exactly like Tripp described you. I'm Bethy," she said in a bubbly voice, and stuck out her hand for me to shake.

I shook her hand, relieved that this was a friend of Tripp's.

"Yes, I'm Della. It's nice to meet you," I replied. I wanted to make friends here. I didn't like being a loner.

"I'm sorry I've not been in to welcome you sooner. Things have been a little crazy. Woods and Jace are best friends. You met Woods, right?"

I only nodded.

"Well, Woods has been over at my place with Jace trying to decide what to do about . . . well, never mind. I'm probably not supposed to talk about his private life with other people. Besides, I doubt you care to hear me ramble. I actually came here for a reason." She paused and flashed me a full smile again. "We're having a little party over at Jace's tonight. Next week kicks off spring break season. It runs from March first through the end of April. This place gets swarmed with people. I want you to come. No, I insist you come. There are people you need to meet. The more people you know, the better. I just wish Blaire was here. She's my best friend and you would love her. She and her fiancé are off dealing with family." She sighed and put her hands on her hips. "So, you coming?"

I had planned on going back to Tripp's condo and taking a walk down the beach and maybe reading a book. But she was right. I needed to meet people.

"Sure. I'd love to. Where and what time?"

Bethy squealed and clapped her hands. "Yay, I'm so glad! Okay, go get changed if you want and come over to Jace's at about eightish. Oh, and he lives . . . you got a pen?" I reached into my purse and pulled out a receipt from the grocery store last night and a pen, then handed them to her.

She scribbled down the directions and handed them back to me.

"See you in a few!" she called out, then spun around and headed back to her car.

I watched her drive away before walking over to my car and getting in. I couldn't get her comment about Woods "dealing with" something out of my head. She was right, she shouldn't have been talking about his personal life, but I was curious. Even though I shouldn't have been.

❀

I had found the right place. Cars were parked everywhere. This was a little intimidating, but then, it was also another experience. I was on this trip for things like this. I parked my car and got out, hoping I had dressed appropriately. I had been torn between dressing to fit in with the members of the club I'd come in contact with for the past two days and dressing to fit in with Bethy. I'd settled for somewhere in between. My blue jean skirt, black leather boots, and vintage Bob Marley T-shirt would hopefully work.

Before I could knock, the door swung open and Bethy was reaching out to grab my hand and pull me inside. "You're here!"

I couldn't reply because she started yelling at someone to stop eating salsa over the white rug. I let her pull me through the crowded house and out onto the back porch. "Sorry, it's so crazy. It's not as bad out here," she said, glancing back at me.

A couple of guys were sitting around a fire pit with beers in their hands. It looked like that was our destination.

"Boys, this is Della. Tripp's friend." She smiled at me, then pointed to an attractive guy who reminded me so much of Tripp I wasn't surprised when she said, "That's Jace." She then pointed to a guy with long blond curls and a mischievous grin. "That's Thad." He winked, and I decided I liked him. He had that "just for fun" look about him. "And this is Grant, who surprised us by showing up. We thought he was up north again." Grant was by far the best looking out of the trio. His dark hair was tucked behind his ears, and he had a twinkle in his eye. The sexy smirk he was sending my way was extremely tempting.

"Hello, Della, why don't you come share my seat? I'll even let you sip from my beer," Grant drawled.

I thought about saying no, but then caught myself and flashed him a smile in return before walking over toward him. "You gonna scoot over, or am I supposed to sit in your lap?" I asked, hoping the teasing in my voice didn't sound stupid.

Grant's smirk grew into a full-blown grin. "Hell yeah, I want you to sit in my lap," he replied.

I was trying to decide if Braden would think this was a bold, fun move or if I was coming off as a slut. I could never tell. She was always my gauge for what I should and shouldn't do. Which was one reason she sent me off to figure out life all by myself.

I might as well go with it now. I'd already acted like a hussy. I stepped over his legs, propped up on the iron rail that went around the outside of the fire pit, and then took a seat in the stranger's lap.

"He won't be here long, baby. You might wanna come over here to this lap. I never leave this place," Thad said from across the fire.

Grant's arm wrapped around my waist and pulled me back against his chest. "You never know, Thad. I might have found a reason to stick around awhile."

I was pretty sure I was in over my head.

"Grant, play nice. She's a friend of Tripp's," Bethy scolded. I wondered if she was thinking I was some kind of cheap whore now.

"Don't go getting all tense in my lap, sweetheart. Lean back and get comfortable," Grant whispered in my ear. His smooth Southern accent made me feel warm. I liked this guy. I managed to relax and do as he said.

"Here, you can have my beer. I'll get another one next time one of these chumps gets up for another round."

I didn't really care for beer. But I also didn't want to be rude, so I took it. "Thanks."

"You're most welcome."

I was surprised that his hands didn't go to my legs but one stayed around my waist and the other was resting on the arm of the chair. I liked that. He wasn't assuming I was easy just because I'd crawled into his lap.

"Tell us about Tripp. We haven't seen him in for-fuckin'-ever," Thad said.

I didn't know much about Tripp. We'd talked on the nights we worked together but we never got real deep with our life stories.

"He's doing good. Women come from miles around just to sit at the bar and flirt with him. He has a dedicated following. He enjoys his job, but after seeing this place, I have no idea why he stays in Dallas."

Thad cut his eyes over to Jace, and they both looked solemn. They obviously knew why Tripp wasn't here and it upset them. They missed him. I didn't blame them. Tripp was a great guy.

"So, why did you come running here from Dallas?" Grant asked as his hand slipped up and covered my stomach. His thumb was awfully close to brushing the underside of my left breast. I wasn't sure if this was okay or if I should just go with it.

"Woods! It's about damn time." Jace's words surprised me, and I wasn't sure I was okay with sitting in Grant's lap anymore. I hadn't expected Woods to be here.

I glanced back at him and my heart stuttered when his dark eyes zeroed in on me . . . or Grant . . . or both.

"I didn't know you were back in town," Woods said to Grant, but his eyes shifted right back to me.

"Yeah, came in last night. Might stick around a little while." The teasing lilt in his voice didn't seem to amuse Woods.

I watched as Woods walked over to me and held out his hand. "Della, would you come with me, please?"

As attractive as Grant was, Woods's dark, commanding

tone was too hard to resist. I slipped my hand in his and he pulled me up out of Grant's lap. I started to say something to Grant, but Woods pulled me back inside the house without a word to anyone else.

"Where are we going?" I asked, setting my beer down on the first table we passed before he made me spill it.

Woods didn't reply. He nodded to the first few people who called out a greeting, but then he just started ignoring them. I had to run to keep up with his fast pace.

We went down a hall, and Woods jerked open the door to the last room on the left and pushed me inside before closing the door behind him.

I was starting to get worried that I'd somehow made him angry when he stalked over to me until he had me pressed back against the wall. The emotions in his brown eyes confused me. He didn't seem angry. He looked confused, torn, and maybe turned on.

"I'm sorry," he finally said as he placed his hands flat against the wall on either side of my head. "I think I may have snapped."

I hadn't been expecting an apology. "Okay," I replied, waiting on more of an explanation.

"I want to be inside you again, Della. I want to pull this sexy-ass excuse for a skirt up and bury myself in the tightest pussy I've ever been in."

Whoa.

Woods lowered his head until his breath was warm against my ear. "It's a real bad idea. Fucking you is all I can think about, but it's a bad idea. Push me away and leave the room. It's the only way I can keep from touching you."

That night we'd spent together was one I still dreamed

about when my dreams were good. How could I walk away when he was offering it again? Why would I want to? I liked Woods. He wasn't just sexy and really good at making me feel wanted. He was thoughtful and well liked by everyone. He was one of the good guys. I needed affection. I had lived most of my life without it. Sex made me feel close to someone even if just for a little while. I'd lost my virginity to a guy who had held me and touched me. I'd wanted to be touched so badly. I'd wanted to feel close to someone. It had been a mistake. The guy hadn't been caring and thoughtful the way Woods was. Having Woods touch me was so different. I craved the way he made me feel.

I moved my hands to his chest and laid my palms against the hard muscles under his shirt that I had licked thoroughly, every wonderful ripple. "What if I don't want to leave? What if I want you to pull my skirt up?" I asked, looking up at him through my eyelashes. It was a simple question. An honest one.

"Damn, baby," he murmured just before his mouth covered mine. The desperation in his kiss made me tingle between my legs. Our tongues danced and tasted until we were both pressing our bodies closer while our hands fought with the clothing between us. I managed to pull Woods's shirt over his head and then covered one of his dark nipples with my mouth and sucked hard. My panties were jerked down and I quickly stepped out of them as he pulled them over my boots.

"You're keeping these boots on. I want it all off but the boots," he growled as he pulled my shirt off and then made quick work of my bra.

As soon as he had me naked, I went back to kissing his chest. Jeffery's chest hadn't looked like this. I had never touched a chest like this but with Woods.

49

Woods's hands circled my waist, and he picked me up and pressed me against the wall as he slammed into me.

"WOODS! YES!" I cried out as the pleasurable pain engulfed me and I wrapped my arms around his neck to hold on.

"Fuck yes . . . fuck yes . . . damn, Della baby, I've fantasized about this since the last time I was up in here. It's like some kind of fucking utopia. I don't want to ever come out."

Woods's breathing was heavy as he leaned over my body and buried his head in my neck. "So good," he groaned.

"Fill me, then you can do it again," I promised, wanting him to move. I craved the orgasm I knew he could give me. That one moment when I couldn't tell where I ended and he began. Bad memories weren't there to haunt me during that nirvana. It was my one moment of relief. I intended to get a lot of those from him tonight. I didn't care about anything else. Just how Woods could make me feel.

Woods let out a crazy growl before he started pumping in and out of me. He licked a trail down my neck and bit me on my shoulder and just above my breast several times. I watched, desperate to get as lost in him as I could. His tongue trailed a path down to my nipple and flicked it several times before pulling it into his mouth. I was so close to coming.

My legs started getting weak from the impending orgasm. Woods noticed and grabbed both my legs and moved us even closer to the wall for support. His eyes lifted, and the moment they locked with mine my pleasure exploded and I cried out his name until it was a whimper.

"Uhh, fuck, Della, uuuh, God yes." Woods's release shook his body so hard it sent a second ripple of pleasure through me. I managed to hold on to him tightly and rested my head against his chest.

Our breathing was hard and heavy. It sounded like we'd both just run a marathon. I *felt* like I'd just run a marathon but had managed to reach heaven in the process.

Woods's hand ran down my hair and my back over and over as we stood there. It was a soothing gesture that only made me like him more. I'd never even been hugged until Braden held me the night I found my mother dead. Woods gave me something no one else had. I sought out affection from others. Not only could Woods give me that but he made everything else fade away. If I could take him home with me at night, would I have my nightmares? Could he exhaust my body with the ability to bring me pleasure until all I could remember was him?

Woods

I was going to take her home with me tonight. I needed more of this. I wanted to taste her again and spend hours rolling those candy-red nipples against my tongue. She was like crack. It had taken all my willpower to walk out on her the last time we'd done this. Now I needed to get her out of my system or at least die trying.

She snuggled deeper into my arms, and her soft, satisfied sigh only made me hard again. Damn, she was all kinds of sweet. I shouldn't have been doing this with her, but my body had other ideas.

I slowly pulled out of her before I got completely hard again. If that happened I'd end up fucking her just like this again, and I needed to change my condom.

"Woods Kerrington, I'm going to kick your ass if you're doing what I think you're doing! You need to get out here. Angelina just showed up." Bethy's angry snarl wasn't missed as she pounded on the door.

Hell! I didn't want to deal with Angelina right now. I wanted to change my damn condom and sink myself back inside Della.

Della leaned back from my embrace and frowned up at me. "Who's Angelina?"

Who was Angelina? Did I lie to her? No. I couldn't. But telling her the truth meant that I wouldn't get to do this again. I needed to find a way to explain it so that I didn't end this . . . this thing we had going.

"Please answer me, Woods," she said as she dropped her legs to the floor and stepped away from me. I felt cold without her. I jerked my pants back up. Her arms crossed over her chest protectively. It only made me want to pull them away so that she wasn't blocking my view.

"Woods?" She was waiting.

I couldn't do it. I could not lie to her just to get her to keep fucking me. *Dammit!* Why did I have to be so honorable?

"She's my soon-to-be fiancée." The words physically hurt coming out of my mouth. The idea of marrying Angelina and never knowing this again almost made me throw all this shit with my dad out the window and say screw it. But I couldn't. It was my future, and Della would leave soon. I couldn't throw my future away for a few weeks of the hottest fuck of my life.

"Soon-to-be?" she asked, reaching for her bra. I wanted to help her put it on, but I knew she wouldn't want me to. Not after I clarified this.

"I'm going to ask her to marry me tomorrow night during the Delamar Benefit at the club."

Della's eyes went wide and she began clumsily trying to put her bra back on as she put more distance between us. "Ohmygod," she whispered, and jerked her shirt over her head. I watched helplessly as she pulled her skirt on and adjusted it. "Ohmygod, I did it again," she murmured, and shook her head in disbelief. When she started for the door, I panicked. This couldn't be it.

"Della, wait. Let me explain," I begged, and she shook her head.

"No, don't. I get it. I'm an easy lay. You're about to tie your-self to a girl for the rest of your life so you used me. One more last night of fun." She let out a hard laugh. "I'm an easy target. I know that. Congratulations on your upcoming nuptials. I hope she says yes."

I couldn't find words to make this right, when she jerked the door open and came face-to-face with a very angry Bethy.

"Are you okay? No, you're not. Come with me," she said to Della in a soothing tone. Then she shot me a glare. "I can't believe you," she snapped.

I watched them both walk away from me. I zipped my jeans, grabbed my shirt, and slipped it on. The pink scrap of fabric I'd jerked off her in my insanity to be in her lay forgotten on the floor. She was walking around in that short skirt with no panties. *Damn.* I picked up the last memory I'd have of knowing just how good Della Sloane felt and tucked it into my pocket.

❈

Grant met me in the hallway. I owed him an apology, too. Not that I was in the mood to give him one. He'd probably be the next one to find out just how amazing Della felt. My blood heated up as images of Grant touching Della flashed in my head.

"What the hell are you doing? I thought you were gonna ask Angelina to marry you tomorrow night. Jace said you have the ring already."

I let out a frustrated sigh. "I am. It's a little deeper than it looks. I hooked up with Della about four months ago when she was passing through town. She's memorable." I wasn't about to tell him just how good she was, because I had no doubt he'd try her out himself, and I knew his heart was too abused to ever love again.

"So you needed one more taste? She know that was what was up? If she did, then that's cool. But if she didn't, then you're a sorry-ass motherfucker." The last part came out in a soft voice laced with an angry threat.

"I'm the motherfucker," I replied, and shoved past him as Angelina made her way toward me. I had her to deal with now.

"I've been looking everywhere for you. Where have you been?" she asked. I started to lie, then I decided she didn't need to think this was a fairy tale. She needed the truth.

"Having really hot, wild sex. If I'm asking you to marry me tomorrow at the benefit, then I needed to have one more fond memory."

Most girls would have flinched, but I'd known Angelina wouldn't. This was a business transaction for her, too.

"I hope it was a good one because I won't allow it once I'm wearing that ring," she hissed.

"It was *incredible*," I replied, and headed for the front door. "Let's go."

Della

I didn't want to go back onto the porch with Bethy. I saw Grant walking toward us and I just wanted out. This time it hurt. With Jeffery I'd just been disgusted. But with Woods . . . it was painful. He had been different. Or at least I'd thought he was different. The way he touched me and wanted me had given me hope. I was silly to think hot sex was the answer to my problems. It had all been selfish. Woods wasn't giving me pure affection. My heart still hurt. I'd wanted that so much.

I felt the edges of my vision starting to blur, and I knew I needed to be alone. This wasn't something anyone needed to see. I didn't want these people to think I was a freak, too.

"I just want to be alone, if you don't mind," I told Bethy, and forced an apologetic smile her way before heading outside into the cool night air. I didn't look back and I didn't try to find my car. I wasn't in any condition to drive. I needed somewhere dark and quiet. Somewhere safe. *I needed somewhere safe*. I chanted the word *safe* in my head as my vision became more and more blurry. I managed to find a house that looked empty and sat down on the back side of it, facing away from the road. I pulled my knees up and tucked my head between them. I could get through this. It was just a symptom of my trauma. Or at least that's what the doctors kept telling me.

Don't go outside, Della. It's dangerous. Your daddy is dead because he went outside. Stay here where it's safe. With me. We'll be safe together. Just the two of us.

I felt tears fill my eyes as my mother's words began tumbling through my head. I tried so hard to repress the memories. But when I was emotionally spent, they came back. They didn't just hide away in my dreams.

Shhh, Della dear. I know you want to ride a bike, but so many bad things can get you outside. You're only safe in here. Remember that. We can't leave or bad things will happen. Let's sing a song, okay? One that is happy. One that is safe.

"No, no, no, Momma. You aren't going to do this to me. I'm stronger than you. I can beat this," I said as I pushed the memories back. I wasn't my mother. I wanted to live life. I wanted to face danger, and I wanted to know all the emotions that went along with it.

I sat there a long time and stared up at the moon. It was something I used to long to see. I knew that at night I could get away from the safety of my house and see Braden. I could ride her bike down the dark streets and I could breathe in the fresh air. The night sky had become my friend.

Finally, I wiped my face with the backs of my hands and stood up. I was okay. I'd made it through this alone. Braden hadn't been here to tell me to breathe and make me laugh while she kept her arm wrapped around my shoulders. This time it had just been me. I was proud of myself.

⚙

I lay awake that night thinking about packing up and leaving, but in the end I decided I was done with running. I couldn't run every time I came in contact with pain or a problem was placed in my path. It was time I reacted like the rest of the world and faced it head-on. However, I might need to find another job. My boss might not want me working for him anymore. I'd just ask him. I would walk right up to him, be very professional, and ask him if I still had a job or if he needed me to look elsewhere for one. That would be easy enough.

If I could keep from remembering how his face looked when he got off. Dangit. That was going to be a problem. Thinking about Woods in a sexual way had to stop. He was my boss. Nothing more.

⚙

The following day I walked in the back entrance of the clubhouse and headed for his office. Might as well address this right away. Get it over with so I wouldn't waste any more time thinking about it.

I knocked on his door and waited. No answer. Crap. I turned and was headed back down the hall toward the kitchen entrance when Woods walked into the building. His eyes locked on me and I stopped. Just seeing him again was hard. I had let our sex become something more. I'd let myself think I needed it. I mentally shook my head to clear it.

"Hello, Mr. Kerrington. I was looking for you. I need to make sure I still have a job or if you'd prefer I resign and go find one elsewhere." That sounded very cool and no-nonsense. I was impressed.

Something I wasn't sure I understood flashed in Woods's eyes. He took a step closer to me and stopped. "You have a job here as long as you want one," he replied.

"Thank you. I appreciate it." I didn't wait for an answer. Instead, I headed for the kitchen entrance and never looked back.

When the swinging doors closed behind me, I let out the breath I'd been holding. I'd done it. We'd had our closure. No more words needed. I could ignore him and he could ignore me.

"Oh, good, I get to work with you instead of Jimmy today. He drives me nuts in the mornings." A girl I'd seen only once before, on my first day, smiled at me as she walked into the kitchen tying her apron around her waist.

"Della, right?" she asked, and pulled her long brown hair up into a ponytail.

"Yes, and you're"—I glanced down at her name tag—"Violet," I replied.

She laughed. "Caught you cheating. But that's okay. We just met once before. I'll take the right-side tables seven through fourteen. You take left-side tables one through six. The right side is a harder morning crowd. A lot of regulars. Don't want to throw you to the dogs just yet."

"Thanks," I replied.

"No problem. I want you to stick around. We can't keep good help."

⁂

I managed to forget only one thing, and it was the apple butter for table three's toast. Luckily, they were good with the slipup and still tipped me 20 percent. Not bad. In Dallas you rarely saw 20 percent tips from men over sixty. I was about to cash out and end my shift when Violet came in smiling.

"You got a hot table. Three of the fab four are sitting at their regular table, number two. Woods isn't with them, so they'll flirt, and Grant's there today, so enjoy. They are so yummy to look at. I gotta run. My tables are clear and Jimmy will be here for the lunch shift."

She bounded out the door and I was stuck there looking out toward the dining room. I wasn't ready to face Grant or any of them just yet. Last night was still too fresh.

I wanted to run again. I had to stop this. I grabbed my tray and pitcher of ice water and made my way out to them. Thad, Grant, and Jace were all talking and not paying any attention to me approaching. Good.

Grant's eyes lifted to meet my gaze and he smiled that slow, sexy smirk thing he had going on. "I'm real glad to see you here this morning," he replied.

He knew. Crap. Did they all know?

"It's my job," I replied. "What can I get y'all to drink?"

"You sure make that uniform look good," Thad replied, leaning forward with his gaze on my chest and not my face.

"Shut up," Grant said, and shot him a disgusted look. "I want some coffee, black."

"Coffee for me, too, but I need two creams and a sugar," Jace replied.

"A tall glass of milk," Thad said.

"Put it in a damn bottle, because he's acting like he needs one," Jace said, rolling his eyes.

"I'll be a baby if she wants me to, a big ol' titty baby," Thad replied with a wink.

"You're an ass." Jace shook his head.

I didn't wait for any more comments. I headed back to the kitchen to fix their drinks. I was positive Thad was not someone I wanted to mess around with. He was cute, but I had a feeling he could get annoying.

When I got back out to their table, Woods had joined them. I kept my smile polite and served the other guys their drinks.

"Mr. Kerrington, what can I get for you, sir?"

I managed to look at him as I asked, but I didn't miss Grant's eyebrows shooting up.

"Coffee, black, please." He barely glanced at me as he said it, and went back to talking to Jace.

"Are the rest of you ready to order?"

Grant leaned forward, and I was thankful to have someone to focus my eyes on. I felt silly trying not to look in Woods's direction.

"I don't know about them, but I'm starving," he replied. "Bring me a burger—medium, loaded, and have Juan put that special sauce on it."

"Same thing for me," Thad piped up.

I forced my attention in the direction of Jace and Woods. Jace looked at me. "Bethy made me a late breakfast, so I'm good with the coffee."

The thought of looking at Woods made my stomach hurt. I hated feeling awkward around him now. But he was my boss. So I held my fake smile and looked his way. "And for you?"

Woods finally met my gaze, but only briefly. "Nothing, thanks, I have a lunch date."

With his fiancée, no doubt. I nodded and headed for the kitchen.

"I so want to tap that," Thad said as I walked away.

"Shut up," Grant snapped.

When I brought Woods his coffee, I managed to get away without any more interaction with him.

Jimmy sauntered in and I breathed a sigh of relief.

"Jimmy, I will give you half my tips today if you change sections with me right now."

Jimmy cocked one of his perfectly plucked eyebrows and stared at me like I was crazy. "Girl, I'm not taking half your tips. What's wrong with the section you're in?"

I didn't want to tell him about Woods. I thought about it a second, then said, "Those guys make me nervous and I don't like waiting on Mr. Kerrington. Please," I finished with a final plea.

He rolled his eyes and tied on his apron. "Fine. We can change sides, but I got one through seven. You get eight through fourteen. You're still new and need to earn more tables."

I nodded. "Of course, thank you."

"I think I'm gonna like you. About time Woods hired another server I like working with."

His praise was nice. I liked feeling as if I fit in.

Woods

I stood at my office window and watched as Della's red car drove away. I could lie to myself and say it was a coincidence that I came to look out the window the same time she was leaving. But I knew her schedule. I knew her shift was over, and pathetically I came here to watch her get in her car and go. I had gotten very little sleep worrying that she would leave without a word after last night.

When I walked into the clubhouse today and she came up to me calling me Mr. Kerrington and making sure she still had a job, I was so damn relieved; I hadn't been able to properly apologize to her before she was walking off.

Then I'd decided it was for the best. No need for us to keep pretending there could be more to this. She was cutting me out and I needed to let her do it. For both our sakes. It was the best way to keep me from caving and begging her for something I couldn't have.

The door opened behind me without a knock, and I didn't have to look to see who it was. Only one person would walk into my office without a knock first.

"Hello, Dad," I said without turning around to look at him. I'd idolized him from the time I was a kid. Now a part of me hated him.

"Woods. I came to make sure plans were still firmly in place for tonight. Howard and Samantha will be here. They're planning on this announcement. Letting Howard Greystone down isn't something I intend to do."

He knew I didn't want this, but here he was still reasserting the importance of it.

"Nothing's changed." Those two words went much deeper than I knew he took them. Nothing had changed. He was still controlling things. I still couldn't stand the idea of being married to Angelina, and he still didn't give a shit.

"Good. Your mother is already planning the wedding with Samantha. They've been planning this wedding since the two of you were young. This isn't just securing our future and the success of what your grandfather built; it is also making your mother very happy. She loves Angelina. This will all work out for the best. You'll see. Left up to your own devices you would have never gotten married." The amusement in his voice was lost on me. There was nothing humorous about the fact that both my parents expected me to sacrifice my happiness for theirs.

"At least someone is happy," I said without emotion.

"When you're married and sitting in your new office looking out over the eighteenth hole, with the title of vice president on your door, you'll be happy, too. Right now you're just sulking like a child who isn't getting his way. I know what you need to be successful, and Angelina Greystone is your answer."

I couldn't look at him. The rage burning a hole in my gut would no doubt be flashing in my eyes. My father's footsteps moved away from me and the door closed behind him. I wasn't sure if I'd ever be able to forgive him for this. Or maybe it was me I would never be able to forgive. What man let another control his life? His future?

⊗

Angelina had circled almost the entire ballroom showing off the ring I'd placed on her finger in front of everyone over an hour ago. She was gushing with excitement, and the entire room was buying it. You would think we were madly in love. I wasn't that good of an actor. I preferred to stand over by the bar and drink shots of whiskey.

"She's a looker. If you're gonna get hitched, at least you picked beauty and money. Surely that's something. You look ready to murder anyone who gets close to you," Jace said as he took up the spot beside me at the bar.

Angelina was beautiful in a cold, classical way. She was elegant and refined and manipulative.

"Can't be happy that I've become my dad's fucking puppet," I replied, and heard the slur in my words. Maybe I'd had too much to drink.

"There's that," he agreed, and picked up my whiskey and finished it off before I could. "Probably need to cut yourself off."

"Probably, but then I'd have to endure this sober."

Jace let out a sigh. "I wasn't going to bring this up, but what happened last night with Della?"

I picked up my empty glass and shook it at the bartender. "Nothing," I lied.

Jace smirked. "That's not what Bethy said. Apparently your shirt was off and your pants were undone."

Hell. Figures Bethy had to tell him the details. "I met Della four months ago. We had a night—a really, really fantastic

65

night. Then she walked back into my life and I lost my damn mind. *That's* what happened."

Jace let out a low whistle. "Shit."

He had no idea. This was all shit—the marriage, my father, the job that should be mine without fucking strings. My life was shit. Then there was Della. Sweet, sexy, fun Della, and I couldn't touch her. She was off-limits to me now. "I don't think I'm gonna ever forget the taste of her." My drunken tongue was loose. It was a good thing Jace was the only one standing around to hear me.

"The job with your dad is worth all this?" Jace asked. I knew he was thinking I was a weak sonofabitch. I wasn't strong enough to break free.

"I'm not Tripp. I can't just leave it all behind. Unlike him, I want this life. I want that job. It's mine, dammit."

Jace nodded and reached out to take the whiskey I'd just been served and was about to down. "I said I was cutting you off. Let's get you out of here for a few minutes. The cool night air might sober you up enough to go speak to guests and actually act like you want this job you're willing to let control your life."

I started to follow him. Getting out of here sounded great. "Where's Bethy?" I asked, looking around for his other half.

"She's with Della in the kitchen, working. She didn't want to come to this tonight and asked if I minded if she worked instead."

Della was in the kitchen? I paused outside the ballroom and looked down the hall toward the door that led to the kitchen. Della was in there. I needed to apologize. Explain. Something.

"I need to go find Della. She needs to understand," I said, turning to head for the kitchen.

Jace's hand clamped down on my shoulder. "No, man. That's a real bad idea. You're engaged and Della is your employee. Draw a line and *stay behind it*."

"I already drew the damn line when I put that ring on Angelina's finger. I just want to explain it to her. She doesn't understand." I'd fucked her, then I'd told her I was getting engaged and she'd run off. I couldn't keep picturing the look on her face. It was killing me.

"Do you think it's gonna do any good? What will it accomplish? Leave the girl alone."

He didn't understand. I shook my head and walked to the kitchen.

"I think Tripp likes her. I think she'll be the reason he comes home. He might not have thought it through when he sent her here, but he had other reasons. He's never let anyone live in his condo before. She's different."

I stopped. My chest ached and my stomach felt as if it were being twisted. Tripp liked Della? He was free to travel the world with her. He didn't have responsibilities or goals in life. He just wanted to be. Just like Della.

I leaned against the wall and stared at the kitchen doors. What good would explaining this bullshit do? Nothing. It was still the same. I wasn't the man she was looking for. We wanted two different things out of life, and amazing sex didn't last forever.

The doors to the kitchen swung open, and my event coordinator, Macy Kemp, came walking out with her hand firmly clasped around Della's wrist, pulling her as she stalked toward me. I opened my mouth to tell her to let Della go, but Macy was already talking.

"The lead singer is allergic to shellfish. No one told me this,

67

Woods. No one. I would have warned him off the dips and salads if I'd known." She shook her head and cursed. "He just left in an ambulance, but the idiot will be fine. I've fixed it; so we should be good." She began walking again and dragged Della behind her. The panicked look on Della's face snapped me out of my confused, tipsy state. I didn't like seeing Della upset, and why the hell was Macy pulling on her like that?

"What are you doing with Della?" I demanded.

Macy looked at Della and then smiled at me. "We need a new lead singer. Band can't play without one. I was in complete disaster mode when I walked in on this one singing in the bathroom while she was washing her hands. The girl can blow."

Not a good choice of words. My slacks suddenly became tighter, and Della's face flushed. I couldn't look away from her. "You're singing?" I asked.

She shrugged.

"Yes, she's singing. What part of 'I heard her singing and I need a lead singer' didn't you understand? First, I've got to get her changed into something more appropriate. No time. Let your father know the band will start up in ten minutes." Macy continued on her way, and Della followed quickly behind her.

"She's singing at what is basically your engagement party," Jace said from behind me. I'd forgotten he was standing there.

"It's not my engagement party," I growled.

"You just got engaged and the whole room is talking about your upcoming wedding. So it's pretty damn close."

"Shut up, Jace."

Della

If there was any possible way I could have gotten out of this without quitting, I would have done it. I had been singing all my life, in my house. But then, that had been to escape my mother and my reality. Not in front of people. I loved to sing, and the mirror and hairbrush had been my companions most of my life while I sang to my pretend audience. That had been fantasy.

I had never been sure my singing was even decent. My mother had loved to hear me sing, but she had never been a good judge of anything.

I had opened my mouth to explain this to the lady who had introduced herself as Macy Kemp, the Kerrington Club event coordinator, but she hadn't let me say much. Instead, she informed the kitchen I was being used elsewhere and began dragging me behind her.

I had expected Woods to stop this insanity when he'd seen us, but he hadn't. He had appeared as confused as I felt, but he hadn't stopped this.

I looked down at the short, clingy silver dress I was now wearing. The dress was backless and the neckline dipped low in the front. I felt bare. In more ways than one.

"They won't be looking at you much. They are too busy in

their little elitist herds. You just sing so they'll have music and can dance if they want to," Macy informed me as she shoved me up the steps toward the skeptical band members. I couldn't say I blamed them.

"You're our replacement?" one asked with a hiss of annoyance in his voice.

"At least they'll be looking at her body and won't hear how bad we sound," another grumbled, and pulled his guitar strap over his head.

"What can you sing, sugar?" an older guy with a balding head asked.

I didn't want to be here. I didn't ask for this. I met each of their angry and annoyed glares with one of my own. I'd heard them earlier. They weren't that good. Who did they think they were, treating me like I was here to screw up their lives on purpose? If their lead singer had paid attention to his allergies, this wouldn't have happened.

I walked past each of them before turning to look at the one who had condescendingly asked me what I could sing. "I can sing anything you throw at me," I replied, then walked out onstage like the diva I was *not*.

The familiar tune of Adele's "Someone Like You" began to play, and I was equally relieved I knew the words and sick to my stomach because the popularity of the song was drawing attention from the guests. I had been hoping to be ignored.

I joined the piano with the first melancholy lyrics.

Instead of looking out at the ballroom, I locked eyes with the piano player. His eyes flashed with approval, excitement, and relief as I sang each line.

Just as I had in my room growing up, I blocked out everything else around me and got lost in the lyrics and the music.

This had been my way of coping with the craziness of my life. I used it now to deal with the reality of my life.

⚸

We moved on to "Ain't No Other Man," the Christina Aguilera version. The fun tune got the room to wake up some. So far I had managed not to make eye contact with Woods, although I knew exactly where he was standing. I could feel his eyes on me.

"Can you harmonize?" the lead guitar asked me.

I nodded, and he looked back at the other members and nodded.

Lady Antebellum's "Just a Kiss" started up.

We had successfully made it to the bridge when I glanced out over the room to see Woods dancing with a tall, elegant blonde. I knew I needed to look away. Seeing him and having an image of him with her on my brain would drive me crazy. But I couldn't. She smiled up at him and talked as he looked over her shoulder at nothing, really. He seemed cold. Nothing like the guy I'd been with.

This time he must have felt my eyes on him, because he turned his head my way and our gazes met. Each word sounded like I was singing to him. I wasn't. I couldn't be. But it felt that way. As the song came to an end, I tore my eyes off him and swore to myself I wouldn't look his way again.

⚸

An hour later I'd conquered everything they'd thrown at me. Even the Bruno Mars songs. The pianist slapped me on the back and beamed at me as I walked off the stage.

"You killed it, sugar," the balding bass player called out.

"Anytime you want to join us, you're welcome. Sure can't

71

sing duets with JJ," the lead guitarist said. I assumed JJ was the lead singer.

I threw one last smile over my shoulder. I wasn't sticking around. I needed to be alone. Watching Woods hold his fiancée had been difficult. She was beautiful and perfect. She'd looked safe in his arms. I understood how that felt. Something about being with Woods made you feel safe. I envied her.

⚝

Spring break was in full swing in Rosemary, and Bethy hadn't been exaggerating. This place was filled up with people. I worked five days a week, and most days I worked two shifts. The money was good and I enjoyed working with everyone. Seeing Woods was easier now.

We managed to treat each other with polite indifference. It hurt sometimes when I thought he was watching me and I'd turn to look at him to find he hadn't been looking my way after all. I wasn't sure why I tortured myself with it. He shouldn't be looking at me. He was engaged. My body, however, wanted him to look at me because it wasn't aware just how off-limits Woods was.

Today I was finally off work, and so was Bethy. We had a day on the beach planned. I was excited about spending the day in the sun. It was warmer now than when I'd arrived a couple of weeks ago. Bethy wanted me to come to her condo because she was on the club's private beach. Fewer people. I'd invited Violet to join us after her lunch shift, and Bethy had mentioned inviting another cart girl, named Carmen, who got off later today, too.

I glanced down at my last text as I pulled up to the condos where Bethy lived.

Down at the beach. I have you a spot saved!

I reached back and grabbed my beach bag, then stepped out of the car. Looking up at the building in front of me, I was in awe. This place was superelite. It was on club property, and I knew after working here a couple of weeks that this place had to cost a fortune. Bethy's cart girl paycheck wouldn't even begin to cover the cost of this. Which meant either she got a deal because she worked there, or Jace helped with the rent. Maybe a little of both.

I walked over to the boardwalk and then down to the warm sand. There were more people out here than I expected. I slipped my sunglasses on and then looked for Bethy. I saw her when she stood up and began waving her arms in the air.

Smiling, I headed down to the two bright, colorful beach towels she had laid out. Then I noticed Jace on the other side of Bethy as she sat back down. I looked around her and saw another towel, but it was empty, although it had obviously been used.

"Glad you made it." Bethy beamed up at me. "This towel is yours. Thad's got that one behind us. He's out in the water."

Thad. I could deal with Thad. I'd have preferred Grant, but Thad would do fine. At least it wasn't Woods. But then, I doubted he came out here to lie on the beach during work hours.

"Thanks for inviting me," I told her as I put my bag down and dug out my sunblock. I'd already put one coating on before I left the condo, but this sun was intense. I felt the need to put more on now that I was out here.

"Don't thank me yet. I hadn't been expecting Thad to join us. You may be wishing you hadn't come. I'm hoping he leaves you alone."

I smiled, thinking that Thad rarely left any female alone. I pulled off my cover-up, folded it, and put it in my bag, then sank down onto the fluffy pink-and-yellow towel Bethy had brought for me to lie on.

"I've never swam in the ocean before," I said as I rubbed the lotion into my skin and watched the people out in the water. "I thought it might still be too cold, but they seem to be enjoying it."

Bethy let out a small laugh. "It's freezing. I won't go near it until mid-May. But a lot of people like it that way. If you've never done it, then go test it out."

That was something I wanted to do. It was a part of living that I wanted to experience. I also wanted to surf, but even with my inexperience I was pretty sure surfing required a lot more wave power. Those waves weren't very high.

"Go on out there and try it. Don't let me stop you," Bethy urged.

I smiled over at her and stood back up to walk the short distance to the water's edge.

The first splash of water to cover my feet was shockingly cold. I managed to stifle my squeal and force myself to stand there. My feet slowly sank into the wet sand, and after a minute or so the water wasn't so cold. I eased in farther and had to stop again once the water crashed across my calves.

"It's easier if you just go all in and get the initial shock over with," a familiar deep voice said from behind me. I guess Woods did make it down to the beach on occasion. I glanced over my shoulder to look at him. I was glad for the safety of my sunglasses.

"Is that so?" I asked.

He was standing on the shore wearing a pair of white board shorts and no shirt. His already dark skin looked even more sun kissed against the white shorts. That was un-fair—to every female on this beach. He needed to wear more clothes.

"The only way to do it. You keep easing in and you will never make it out there."

Why was he talking to me today? He'd acted as if I didn't exist since the night he'd told me he was getting engaged. Why now? I looked back out at the water and tried not to think about the way his abs glistened in the sun thanks to tanning oil. He was an engaged man now. Dirty thoughts of him were prohibited.

"You want me to go with you?" he asked, and his voice was closer. Jerking my gaze back around, I saw him taking several more steps in my direction. What was he doing?

"Probably not a good idea. I'll do this alone," I managed to choke out.

"You ever been in the ocean?" he asked as his arm brushed my shoulder. He was too close now.

"No," I whispered, wishing he'd back away. Far, far away.

I heard Woods's swift intake of breath and glanced up at him. His eyes were on my body. Even though he had on dark sunglasses, I could feel his heated gaze on me. Not good. Really, not good.

"Damn, baby. Where's the rest of your swimsuit?"

The rest of my swimsuit? I turned my attention to my body to make sure it was properly covered. What did he mean? I wasn't missing anything.

"This is my swimsuit," I replied.

75

Woods's head lowered, and his mouth was too close to my ear. "That top is barely covering you up," he whispered.

Annoyed, I glared at him. "If you don't like it, then don't look," I replied, and started moving out deeper into the water. Getting distance from him was more important than adjusting to the cool temperature.

"I didn't say I didn't like it. I fucking love it. That's the problem."

I stopped moving. Why would he say that? Did he not care what he was doing to me?

"You can't say things like that to me. It's wrong," I replied angrily.

Woods moved toward me again and I waited. This was a confrontation he wanted to have. I was going to let him have it.

"You're right. I shouldn't. But would you rather I lied? I've done a lot of things to you, Della, but I haven't lied. I don't want to lie to you. I could tell you that I don't care about you or that I don't want you but that would be a lie. You want the truth? Because the truth is, all I can think about is being with you again. I try not to look at you because all I can think about is hauling you off to the first closet I can find and kissing every inch of your body." He was breathing hard and his jaw was working back and forth.

Why? If he wanted me like that, then why was he engaged to someone else? Shaking my head, I crossed my arms protectively over my chest. "I don't understand you."

He smirked and shook his head. "No one does. But I'd like to explain it to you. Please. Just go have a drink with me. I need you to understand this."

His tactic was different, but he was the same. He wanted me for an amusement. Someone to entertain him for a mo-

76

ment and then he'd find another. I wasn't that girl. I shook my head and started to leave the water. I wanted the safety of the beach.

"You won't even let me explain?" he called out.

I looked back at him. "The ring on her finger is the only explanation I will ever need."

Woods

There were orders I needed to make that Juan, the head chef, had placed on my desk yesterday. Phone calls I needed to return and a fiancée determined to get me to decide on a date for our wedding. Was I doing any of those things? No. I was torturing myself instead.

Della needed a bigger bikini top, and Thad was about to lose the use of both his hands. Grinding my teeth, I tore my eyes off Thad rubbing sunblock on Della's back and shoulders. Thad had managed to get her to go into the water with him. I had sat here and watched every agonizing second of it. Her squeals of laughter and Thad's need to keep touching her had jealousy raging through my veins. I had no right to be jealous. We'd had hot sex. That was it. I knew nothing else about her. But I wanted to.

I wanted to know where she was from. It was obviously the South. I wanted to know if she had brothers and sisters. Who gave her those blue eyes that I'd seen glazed over with pleasure? Did she like to dance? Where had she learned to sing like that? She'd completely blown me away at the Delamar event. There was so much I'd never get a chance to know.

"Your shoulders are looking pink. I'd have thought with your complexion that you'd be used to the sun," Thad said, and I couldn't keep my eyes from shifting back to look at her shoulders. He was right; they were pink.

I stood up and walked over to the rental stand.

"Give me an umbrella," I told the young guy I'd hired only two weeks ago, before the spring break rush hit.

"Yes, sir." He nodded. "You want me to go put it in the sand for you, too, sir?"

No. I wanted to do this myself. "I got it. Thanks."

I took the umbrella. My eyes locked with Della's when I turned to walk back that way. She was watching me curiously. Thad was saying something in her ear but she wasn't paying attention to him. Her complete focus was on me.

"Move," I ordered Thad, giving him little time to actually follow my command before shoving the umbrella pole into the sand and starting the circular motion it took to get it to burrow deep enough so that it stood up and didn't fly away.

"The umbrella isn't gonna reach you from there," Bethy said with a smirk.

"Didn't get it for me."

"Oh, you got it for me? How sweet, but I'm working on a tan," Bethy replied, thoroughly enjoying herself.

"Then move over. Della's shoulders are pink." There, I'd said it. Bethy had wanted me to admit it, so I had. Let Della think about that one for a minute.

"You got it for me?" Della asked. I could hear the surprise in her voice, and I didn't look up at her until I had the umbrella secure.

"Yeah" was my only response before I walked over and picked up my towel. It was time I left. She didn't want me here and I shouldn't be.

"Thank you," she called out as I started to leave. I nodded without looking her way.

"You leaving?" Jace asked.

"I have some work to do."

"Don't forget Friday night at the Sun Club," Bethy said, grinning up at Jace, who chuckled and shook his head.

It was Jace's birthday and Bethy was determined to celebrate it with a night of partying at the only club in town. She'd rented out the place with a little help from Grant, who was friends with the owner. It was invite only.

"Wouldn't miss it," I replied.

�֍

A night of drinking, dancing, and karaoke was not something that interested Angelina. But at least I'd done my duty and invited her. She'd quickly said no and made up the excuse that she needed to fly to New York to get fitted for her wedding dress. That would take a few days, so I was all for it.

Bethy had gone all out on the decorations. Shot glasses had been glued to the back of a large piece of wood to spell out "twenty-four." There was a small light in each shot glass, so the effect was pretty damn cool. I spoke to a few people as I passed, but I was scanning the room for Della.

I was going to try and talk to her one more time tonight. Watching her laugh and talk to Thad and Grant like they were old friends was about to kill me. I wanted that, too. I knew she wasn't seeing either one of them, but they were getting to know her. Grant had said something about Della wanting to learn to golf, and I'd been instantly jealous that he knew something personal about her. Something I didn't know.

"You know, Woods, once you get engaged, it's expected for you to show up with your fiancée to events," Bethy said as she stopped in front of me and held out a shot of something that looked like whiskey.

"She had to go to New York," I replied, and took the glass from her hand.

"Hmmm, interesting," Bethy drawled, then walked away.

I downed the shot and set the glass on the bar. Della came walking out of the ladies room, and I took a minute to appreciate her tiny blue jean shorts and those boots I'd seen on her once before. I knew exactly how she looked in nothing but the boots. The black lacy top she was wearing was strapless, and when she raised her arms even a little, a small sliver of her stomach would show.

The girl sure knew how to dress to drive a man insane.

"Stop lusting, bro. You sealed your fate already," Grant said with a chuckle as he walked up to me.

"I'm not married yet," I muttered, and shot him an annoyed glare before looking back at Della.

"No, but you will be. If you'd wanted Della more than the VP job, you'd already have her. You made that choice, and I've known you long enough to know you're sticking with it."

"It's more complicated than that."

Grant crossed his arms over his chest and stared at me. "Really? How so?"

I didn't want to explain to him how I felt about Della. This wasn't his business. He of all people should know what it feels like to want someone you know is a really bad idea. He'd been there, done that, and gotten burned. He just didn't know that I knew about it. He thought it was a big secret. Nothing with Nannette was a secret. Ever. His former stepsister was all kinds of fucked-up evil. He'd known that most of his life. This thing I had with Della was different but just as impossible.

"You know how complicated things can get, Grant. I know you do," I said in a low voice meant only for his ears.

Grant's eyes narrowed, then he smirked, although it wasn't an amused one. More of a disgusted one. "Who told you?" he asked.

No one had told me. I'd watched it happen. Not much went on in my club that I didn't see or hear about. "No one else knows. I saw it. I don't think anyone else did."

Grant's face looked sour. "It's over."

I nodded. "I figured. No one can stay close to her for long."

We stood in silence and both watched Della. When her eyes finally turned and met mine, I decided to make my move. We were talking tonight. I wasn't letting her blow me off again. Not this time.

Della

I shouldn't have looked at him so long, but I hadn't been able to keep pretending he wasn't staring at me. In a weak moment, I met his steady gaze and saw the sadness in his eyes. He had secrets hidden inside. I knew what that felt like. The stupid part of me wanted to reach out and help him.

Luckily the smart, rational part of me knew he was walking this way and I needed to move. He would want to explain again. I didn't need his explanation. I understood. Tonight was about having fun with new people. Not me running off to find a dark hole to hide in if my crazy started to break through.

I made it only two steps before his large hand wrapped around my upper arm. "Please, Della. Don't. I just want to talk."

Again with the sadness. It was even in his voice. He was hurting somehow. I'd hurt for so long all alone. Identifying pain in others was easy for me. I was drawn to it in some strange, perverse way.

"What do you want, Woods?" I asked without looking at him.

"To talk. I just want to talk."

He wanted to talk. Fine. We could talk if it would give him some closure. Maybe ease that sadness in his eyes that haunted me. "Okay. But we talk in here." Being alone with him wasn't going to happen.

83

"Fair enough," he replied.

I finally turned around and stared up at him. He really was beautiful. Sometimes it was easy to ignore. But up close, when he was completely focused on me, it was harder. I'd seen those eyes glowing with passion. I knew what his mouth tasted like and I had heard his cries of pleasure. I never would again, but those memories were hard to forget.

"Come sit with me," he said, gently pulling my arm toward an empty table in the corner.

I took the seat across from him, putting the safety of the small cocktail table between us. He had something he wanted to say, and the sooner he said it, the sooner I could get away from him.

"What is it you want to talk to me about?" I asked.

Woods ran his thumb over his bottom lip thoughtfully, and I jerked my eyes away from his face. I didn't want to look at those lips and remember.

"About the other night. I was trying to be honest with you, and I screwed it up. I shouldn't have let you leave without explaining everything to you."

I knew sitting down that this was the only thing we had to talk about. It still didn't ease the pain that came with it. I had been so open and free with him. And no, he hadn't been honest.

"If you had been honest, you wouldn't have had sex with me before telling me you were about to get engaged. I didn't even know you were in a relationship. And one so serious! Were you with her back when we . . . the night we . . . met?"

He rested both his elbows on the table and leaned forward.

"No. I wasn't. It isn't a real relationship, Della. Not like you think it is. It's a business deal. Her father's company merging with my father's. We aren't exclusive . . . or we weren't until I gave her the ring."

A business transaction? What? "I don't understand," I finally replied.

Woods let out a soft, bitter laugh. "You wouldn't because it's screwed up. My grandfather built the Kerrington Club. It's been successful down here, but it isn't in the big leagues. The Greystone name being joined with the Kerrington name would open doors for my father . . . and me, that couldn't be opened before."

Greystone? Where had I heard that before? "Your fiancée is a Greystone?" I asked, trying to understand what he was telling me.

"Yeah, she is the only heir to the Greystone name. Her father and mine see this as a winning solution for them both. I will one day control not only Kerrington but the Greystone empire as well."

Wow. So people really did marry for reasons as shallow as this. Is that why he seemed sad? "Does she make you happy?" I asked, watching his face for any sign of an answer instead of listening to just his words.

"No. But she wants this arrangement as well," he replied. The regret etched in his face hurt my heart. I didn't like that he'd had sex with me without telling me all this, but I still didn't want him to be so sad. We only got one life and that was it. I knew that better than most. I'd lost the first part of my life locked away. He would lose the last part in a very similar situation. His heart would be locked away. Unused.

"This is what you want?" I finally asked.

He didn't reply right away. Instead he stared at me intensely. My heart picked up its pace and I realized it always would around Woods. He had connected with it and I couldn't stop that. I had tried.

"Yes, and no. I want what I've grown up knowing would be mine. I want to take my rightful place in my family's business. I've worked hard for this. But . . . I don't want Angelina."

His eyes said more than they should have. I dropped my gaze and stared at my hands resting in my lap. I had a decision to make. I could continue to push Woods away, or I could forgive him. I could be his friend. Nothing more. He'd given me a job when I needed one. I would leave soon. Until then, maybe I could share memories and moments with Woods. We could find the happiness in life together. New experiences. His last taste of freedom and my first taste.

Lifting my eyes, I met his steady gaze. He was waiting on something from me. "Can we be friends? Even after everything else? We could just start over," I suggested.

The muscles in Woods's neck moved as he swallowed. I wondered if I'd read him wrong. If he had just been needing closure and nothing more. But his eyes said something different. "I'd like that."

Smiling, I reached my hand out toward him. "Hello, I'm Della Sloane."

A crooked grin touched Woods's perfect face and he slipped his hand into mine. "Woods Kerrington. It's nice to meet you, Della."

His warm touch caused me to shiver, and I pulled my hand away and stood up. "I'm going to get a drink. Save me a dance tonight."

He nodded. "Without a doubt."

Bethy met me at the bar. I had planned to take a deep, calming breath after getting far enough from Woods to think this through. But instead I managed to smile at her like nothing was wrong.

"Can I ask what the handshake was about?" Bethy said, sitting down on the stool beside me and ordering two lemon-drop shots.

"We're starting over. This time I know he's engaged and we're going to be friends."

Bethy nodded, but I could see the disbelief in her eyes.

"Really, we are. Nothing more," I assured her.

The bartender slid the pale yellow drinks our way.

"I believe that you believe that. But Woods doesn't want Angelina. So you see, if I'm skeptical about him keeping it friendly between the two of you, I have reason."

Even Bethy knew he didn't want to marry Angelina. I didn't understand this. Would it be so bad not to connect his name with hers?

"It just seems like he's sacrificing his happiness for money and gain. I don't think that will end well."

Bethy threw back her shot and then wiped a drop off her bottom lip with the pad of her thumb. "It will be a disaster. He'll be miserable. But he thinks this is what he wants out of life. No one can convince him otherwise. In their world of money and power this is what they do. It's why Tripp took off running. He didn't want to play that game."

Tripp? He'd had that kind of ultimatum, too? But he'd left. He'd run. He hadn't sacrificed his happiness. He was living. There was no cage holding him in. Cages were suffocating. I hated the idea of Woods living in one.

"I'm just passing through. While I'm here, I think we can be friends. I like him. I want to get to know him. When I have his memory to pull out one day and think about, I don't want it to be just the sex. I want to know the man. Is that wrong?"

Bethy picked up my lemon drop and handed it to me. "No. It's not. Now, drink up. I need someone to get the karaoke going and—tag, you're it."

I shook my head. "Oh, no. Not me."

Bethy nodded. "Yes, you. I've heard about your amazing vocal skills. It's time I heard them. Come on, do it for *me*. Please."

I took the shot glass and quickly downed the tangy drink.

Woods

Grant took Della's seat when she walked away.

"I take it that means you two made amends," Grant said as he put his beer down on the table.

"We're friends," I replied. Not real sure how that was going to work, but I was going to make certain it did.

"Friends," Grant replied, and nodded as if he agreed. The look on his face was amused, though. "Good luck with that."

His comment pissed me off, but he was right. I needed all the luck I could get. Keeping a straight head around her was going to be hard.

"Thanks."

Grant chuckled. "Looks like you think that's as impossible as I do."

I'd started to respond when Bethy walked up on the stage. "It's time for some karaoke. Now that you've all had some free liquor, you can sing for your drinks. Don't worry, I won't make you come up here, yet. You have an entire song to drink enough, until coming up here sounds like a good idea. Della has agreed to sing first because she doesn't have to be drunk to sound badass."

I shifted my eyes to Della, who was looking up at Bethy like she wanted to crawl under a table. I wanted to go save her from this, but I sure as hell wasn't about to go sing. I'd never live it down.

"I got this," Grant said, and jumped up. I watched him saunter over to Della and say something that made her beam up at him. Stupid fucker. What was he doing?

Della slid her hand into his and they walked up to the stage together. He was gonna sing with her. He hadn't sung in front of a crowd since high school.

Della looked relieved not to be up there alone.

The lyrics to "Picture" by Sheryl Crow and Kid Rock came up on the screen. He was going with a Kid song. Not surprising; he always liked singing Kid Rock songs.

The familiar music began pouring through the speakers. Grant's voice joined it, and I let myself watch Della. She was impressed with his singing. Most people were. Until they heard Rush Finlay sing. Rush and Grant were stepbrothers once for a few short years. But it had been enough to bond them. I never understood why Rush didn't sing anymore, because it had drawn the girls for miles when he was younger. Maybe it was the fact that he didn't want to be his father. He didn't want to be compared to him. Rush's father was the famous drummer from Slacker Demon.

Grant hadn't minded using his vocal skills to attract the girls, though.

Della began her part of the song, and the room went quiet. She was amazing. I'd been completely floored when she'd opened her mouth to sing at the Delamar Benefit. This was one of the things I wanted to know more about. She had to have been singing for a long time.

"I'm just throwing this out there. I'm making a move on her. Your ass is engaged. So you can get all pissed and shit, but I'm still making a move. She's hot and completely worth the ass kicking," Thad informed me. I glared at him as he sat down across from me and shrugged before looking back up at the stage.

She was too smart to get mixed up with Thad. He wasn't her type.

"If she doesn't end up in Grant's bed tonight. He's looking like he's ready to move in on her."

I watched Grant as they finished the song and he pulled her into a hug. My hands clenched tightly into fists. What was he doing?

"Bud, you look like you need reminding you got your stupid ass engaged," Thad said, standing back up.

Della's hands were resting on Grant's arms just a little too comfortably and long. Della's gaze left Grant's face, and her eyes found me. Immediately her hands fell from his arms and she stepped away from Grant after flashing him one more smile. Then she turned and left the stage.

I watched her as she made her way through the crowd. She was headed for the back hallway that led to the restrooms. I didn't think about it too hard. I just went with it. Standing up, I followed her.

She had already disappeared into the restroom when I got back there, so I waited. I wasn't sure what I was going to do. We'd just agreed to become friends, so pushing her back into that small one-stall bathroom and taking her up against the wall again wasn't a good idea. I was positive she wouldn't be so willing anymore. Which burned like acid down my throat. I'd had her. I could have had more.

Staring at the door, I decided this was a bad move. Another mistake. I shouldn't have been back there. I wanted to get to know Della, and this wasn't the way to do it. She'd push me away if I even attempted anything.

I stalked back down the hallway, away from the temptation.

"Woods?" Della's voice stopped me. I couldn't go back there. I looked at her over my shoulder.

"Hey. You did great up there. Sheryl Crow is hard to sing."

She blushed. "Thank you. It was fun. I was nervous when Bethy asked me to, but I'm glad I did."

"I'm glad you did, too."

She walked toward me. "How about that dance now?"

I wanted to dance with her. I wanted that memory. That experience. I held out my hand to her and she placed hers in mine. I stared down at her small hand, and my chest felt like it was stretching. The tightness that surrounded me only grew stronger as I closed my hand around hers and led her out to the dance floor.

I could feel eyes on me, but right now I didn't give a shit. They could look. They could judge me. This was what I wanted, and until I said "I do," I was going to spend time getting to know Della. If I didn't, I'd regret it for the rest of my life.

Jimmy had taken the mic and had just started singing "Wanted" by Hunter Hayes. I was thankful for the slow song. That meant I'd get to pull her closer.

Della slid her hands up my arms and rested them there. She didn't slip them behind my neck and press close to me.

"You smell good," she said, so softly I almost missed it.

"Not as good as you smell, trust me," I replied, and she tensed as my hands tightened their grip on her waist. "It's the truth, Della. I've told you before that you smell incredible. Don't get all uptight because I'm being honest."

She relaxed a little. "Okay, you're right. No harm in thinking your friends smell good." The teasing tone in her voice was cute.

"Is there a rule that says since we're friends you can't wrap your hands around my neck?"

Della paused a moment, then her hands slid up and rested on my shoulders. "I'm not tall enough for them to go any farther. Even in these boots."

"This is good," I assured her, and pulled her closer. "Where are you from, Della Sloane?"

She laughed. "You could easily look on the application you had me fill out to find that information."

She was right. I could. "But I want to hear it from you. I don't want to read it off your file."

Della tilted her head to the side and studied me a moment. "Macon, Georgia."

I'd have guessed Alabama or Georgia. Her accent was thick. "Do you have brothers or sisters?"

A melancholy look came over her face, and she shook her head. "No." That simple "no" sounded like so much more. She wasn't telling me something.

"You don't seem like an only child. The carefree, travel-the-world choice of yours is more like something the baby of a family would do."

Della smiled, but it was one that held secrets. I wondered if I'd ever know those secrets.

"I'm not carefree. Not even close. But I want to be. I'm hoping one day I'll know what that feels like. Right now I'm trying to find me. You know what you want out of life, I don't. I have no idea."

What I wanted out of life? Did I know? Was it even the same anymore? "I know a lot less than you think I do."

93

She smirked. "Is that so?"

Kissing those sexy little lips was tempting. Oh, so tempting. "When's your birthday?" I asked instead of responding to her remark.

Della sighed and looked away from me. "April sixth. When is yours?"

"December tenth. What's your favorite color?"

She giggled. "Blue. Pale blue. What's yours?"

"A month ago I would have said red, but I've changed my mind. I like blue now, too."

"Why?" She cocked an eyebrow and gazed up at me.

I wasn't about to tell her it was because her eyes were blue. She'd get all tense on me again. "A guy can change his mind. I'm allowed to like blue now." I didn't give her time to think about that. "Who was your first-grade teacher?" I asked quickly to distract her. Della stopped dancing and backed away from me. Her eyes appeared almost glassy. Had I said something wrong? Had she figured out why I said blue was my favorite color?

"I need a drink," she said with a wobbly, nervous smile, then darted off away from me.

How could I have upset her by asking her about her first-grade teacher? There was something deep in her eyes that told a story I feared I'd never know.

Della

It was a simple question. Sweet, really, that he'd even care. Had anyone ever cared about such trivial things concerning me before? I had never been asked such innocent personal questions. But he'd asked about my teacher and all I could see was my mother.

Sit here, Della. Don't look out the window. You have to do this work. To be smart you need to read Shakespeare. He will remind you how dangerous the world can be.

I shook my head to clear the memories. I couldn't do this here. Not now.

It's dark out there, Della. Bad things are in the dark. Lock your windows and doors and stay tucked in tight. The monster under your bed will hear you if you get up.

No, Momma. Go away.

Della, don't go outside again tonight. The bad is out there waiting on you. Stay with me. Your brother worries about you. He doesn't want you hurt. Be safe in your bed.

"Della, are you okay?" Strong arms were pulling me close. I went willingly. I needed to be away from her. I didn't want to remember that night. I knew I would if she stayed in my head too long.

"I've got her. Move." Woods's voice sent warmth through me. I was breaking free from the memories. They weren't taking me this time.

Cool night air brushed my face, and I realized I was being carried. I took a deep, calming breath and the tightness in my chest was gone. Woods had brought me out of it. I hadn't been left to remember alone.

I blinked several times and my eyes came back into focus. The darkness was gone.

Woods sat down on a bench along the beach boardwalk and kept me firmly in his lap. "You're back," he said simply.

I nodded. I wasn't sure what to say. I didn't want to tell him what had just happened.

"Good," he said, and brushed my hair out of my face with his free hand. He still held me cradled against his chest with his other.

"Thank you."

Woods's mouth was in a tight line. He was concerned. I'd scared him. I started to sit up, but he held me tighter. "You're not getting up until you tell me something."

My stomach knotted up. I'd never told anyone other than Braden, and she knew why. I couldn't tell Woods. I didn't talk about it.

"You don't have to tell me why that just happened. But does it happen often?"

This wasn't a fair question. Telling him the truth without telling him about my past would only make him think I was crazy. Maybe I was. No one was sure yet. I could be. . . . She was crazy. I could be, too. It was my greatest fear, that I'd snap one day, too. Just like she had. I wanted to live life because if that day came, I wanted to have lived once.

"They're triggered by certain things," I told him, and moved to get out of his arms again. He let me go this time. I was grateful and yet wished he had fought to hold me longer. Because I needed affection from someone after I had these episodes. It helped me recover quicker.

"I triggered it?" he asked.

I shrugged and looked out at the gulf instead of at him. His question had triggered it. I wasn't going to tell him that, though.

We sat there in silence for a few minutes. I knew his mind was running through all kinds of possibilities, and none of them would be accurate.

"I want to know you, Della. I don't want to stop asking you questions. Next time maybe you can ask me questions that you don't mind me asking you. That way I won't ask the wrong thing."

He wanted to know me. My chest felt like it might burst. Tears stung my eyes and I blinked them back. I couldn't cry on him now. "Okay," I replied hoarsely.

Woods's hand reached over and covered mine, holding it firmly in his. He didn't look at me. His eyes stared straight ahead at the waves crashing on the shore. When his fingers threaded through mine, I let them. That simple touch was all I needed. Being here with him pushed back all the darkness. All the pain and sorrow was forgotten. I was okay. It felt good.

"Woods? Is she okay?" Bethy's voice called out, and we both turned to look back at her walking out of the club and toward us.

"She thinks you had too much to drink," Woods said quietly beside me. I hadn't considered what everyone else might think of my episode.

"I'm fine," I told her as she walked up to us.

"Oh, thank God. I was sure I'd made you sick with those lemon shots. They can be fierce if you aren't used to them."

"She just got overheated. That mixed with the alcohol. The cool air brought her around," Woods explained for me.

Bethy's relief was all over her face. "Thanks, Woods. I can stay with her if you want to go back inside."

Woods's hand tightened around mine. "No, I'm good right here. I needed a break, too."

Bethy looked worried but finally nodded and went back inside.

Once she was gone I glanced up at Woods. He was watching me. "Thank you for your help tonight. If you hadn't stepped in that could have been really embarrassing."

Woods's frown was etched with concern. "I'm glad I was there. What's bothering me is the fact that you're traveling all alone. What happens when you're by yourself and this . . . this happens? Who helps you then?"

No one. I managed. "I normally get away before it hits me hard, and I deal with it."

Woods pulled my hand closer to his leg, and instead of saying more or arguing with me about that being a bad idea, he turned his attention back to the dark water.

Woods

You need to get back into Jace's party, and I think I'm going to go back to the condo. I'm tired." Della's soft voice broke into my thoughts.

I wanted to keep her here with me so I could watch her and make sure she was okay. But I knew that wasn't an option.

"I'll drive you. Grant and I will get your car back to the condo for you later." I wasn't letting her drive back alone tonight. For my own sanity I needed to see her safely inside.

"You don't have to do that. I'm okay. Really I am," she argued, letting go of my hand and standing up.

She might have been okay, but I wasn't. "I'm driving you," I repeated, and stood up to tower in front of her. "Please. I'll worry all night if you don't let me."

A smile touched her pink lips and she nodded. "All right. Thank you."

I put my hand on the small of her back because I needed to touch her somehow. The connection reminded me that she was fine now. I led her to my truck and helped her get in on the passenger side. The memory of throwing her inside once before only served to make me even more obsessive in keeping her safe.

She wasn't mine and she never would be, but that didn't

change the way I felt. I'd become possessive of her. I wanted her safe and happy. Tonight had scared the shit out of me. Something wasn't right with Della. The desire to fix it for her was strong and impossible to ignore. What could have happened to her to make her withdraw like that? She'd been completely unresponsive. Like she was just checked out.

Once I was inside the truck, I glanced over at her to make sure she was buckled up. Seeing her strange episode tonight was going to haunt me. I wasn't sure how the hell I was supposed to move on after that.

"Thanks for your help tonight. I hope I didn't freak you out too bad," Della said, glancing over at me.

I needed to respond, but what should I say? *You're welcome and you completely fucked with my head?* I couldn't say that, but I needed to say something.

"I'll always help you, but I'm not going to lie to you. After tonight, I'm concerned. I don't want to drop you off and leave you alone in that damn condo. I want to take you back to my place and take care of you."

I chanced a quick peek at her before looking back at the road. She was biting her bottom lip nervously. She didn't say anything right away. I waited for her to say something. Anything. But she remained quiet. I tried not to think about it and that was proving impossible. I was never going to get the image of her face out of my head.

"I have to learn to live on my own. Live without help. That's why I'm on this road trip. I need to find myself and make a life for me . . ." She trailed off before finishing.

Who told her she needed to figure out how to handle this by herself, and what the fuck had happened to her to make her like this?

100

I reached over and grabbed her hand. "Call me. Any time. If you need someone, call me."

She nodded. Her hand flipped over in mine and she squeezed it. "Thank you."

I pulled in front of Tripp's condo wishing I'd taken a longer route. Della slipped her hand from mine and opened the door.

"I had fun dancing," she said before stepping out of my truck and closing the door behind her. I waited until I saw her safely inside the condo before pulling away.

✖

My mother had called me three times already this morning. I had promised to come to their beach house for a Sunday lunch with the Greystones and apparently she didn't trust me to show up. When my cell phone started ringing in my pocket again, I intended to ignore it. I was on my fucking way to their beach house. She needed to back the hell off.

The fact that it could be Della had me caving in and pulling out my phone. Jace's name lit up the screen.

"Hello."

"Where are you?"

"Going to my parents' beach house for lunch. Why?"

"Because I came by your office and you weren't there. I thought maybe you were playing a round of golf."

"No. Not today."

Jace cleared his throat and I knew there was something more he wanted to say. This wasn't just about me playing golf.

"I, uh, I just talked to Tripp. He's on his way home. I think it's because of her."

Her being Della. *Shit.*

"Okay," I replied, not sure what he wanted me to say.

"They'll both be staying in his condo."

I hadn't thought about that. Della sharing a condo with Tripp? Hell no.

"I don't think I'm okay with that," I said through clenched teeth.

Jace sighed heavily. "Come on, man. You're engaged. You can't have her. If Tripp wants her, you know he'd take good care of her. Just back off and let him have his chance. This may bring him home."

Images of Della's perfect naked body splayed out on a bed for Tripp made me want to go grab him and slam him up against the wall. She was mine. No, she wasn't. Dammit all to hell!

"I need to go," I growled before hanging up and chucking my phone against the car door while I let out a frustrated roar.

Della

The lunch shift was brutal on Sundays. I thought that only in Macon, Georgia, did everyone with a pulse attend church. I was wrong. This was a Southern thing. At exactly 12:05 p.m., the floodgates opened and every table in the dining room became full, with a wait at the door.

I had wondered why I hadn't been put on the lunch shift for Sunday before now. This explained it. This was pros only. I leaned against the wall in the kitchen and pushed the fallen hair out of my face. Somehow we'd survived. The last table was just finishing up and paying their tab.

"The only good thing about Sundays is the tips. I swear I'm gonna quit every week when it's over. Then I count my money," Jimmy said with a wink, and pulled out the roll of money he had tucked in his pocket.

"That was crazy," I agreed.

Jimmy chuckled. "Yep. Good thing is, it's over. You can go home."

Home. Tripp's condo wasn't my home. And today I wasn't sure I was staying there any longer. I hoped my tips were really good, because I might need to pack up and hit the road. Tripp had called last night to let me know he was headed home to visit. I didn't know if that meant he wanted me to move on out now. Or if he was expecting us to share the condo.

I had bad dreams, and many nights I woke myself up screaming. Sharing the condo with Tripp didn't sound like the best idea. But leaving Rosemary didn't sound appealing, either. I liked it here. I liked Bethy and Jimmy and I liked . . . Woods.

"Girl, stop frowning. It's quitting time," Jimmy said in a teasing voice as he walked by me and tossed his apron into the dirty basket.

I managed a smile and nodded. "I think I need a nap," I replied, and took off my apron, too. I wouldn't be getting a nap. There was a good chance that Tripp would be there when I got back. If not, he would be later today.

"I got a hot date. No time for sleeping. See you tomorrow morning," Jimmy called out as he left the kitchen.

I followed him. Once I was outside the clubhouse, I pulled my hair out of the bun I'd twisted it up into and let it hang free. It was giving me a headache. I wasn't used to having my hair pulled back so tightly.

The sound of a car door slamming caught my attention and I turned around to see Woods's truck parked in his reserved space. His fiancée was stalking around the back of the truck with fire in her eyes.

"Just one meal, Woods. Really? You can't play nice for one goddamn meal? What is wrong with you? Am I that abhorrent to you that you can't even be civil to me in front of our parents?" Her loud, shrill voice carried across the parking lot. This was not my business, and I needed to get in the car and leave. But I couldn't. My eyes were locked on Woods as he stepped out of the truck. He looked annoyed.

"You got what you wanted. You, and our fathers, won. I

caved in and agreed to this. But I don't want it. I will never want it." Woods's bored voice was almost too low for me to hear. If I hadn't been so focused on him, I might not have heard his hard reply.

"Really? Well, then, you don't have to have it. Because as much as I want this thing between us to work and as much as I want a husband who will be an asset to the Greystone name, I do not want to live with a man who hates me. I can do better than that. I'm a fantastic catch, Woods Kerrington. I don't need you," she spat out. Her body was trembling with anger.

I felt sorry for her. She was right. No woman deserved this. The unmoved expression in his eyes looked annoyed if anything.

"You're right. I'm sorry. I've just had a lot on my mind today. I shouldn't have acted the way I did at lunch. My dad pushes my buttons the way no one else can. What I said and how I acted was not because of you but because of him."

My heart hurt. The flash of sadness in his eyes had been there for only a moment, but I'd seen it. I wanted to hug him and make the sadness go away. But I couldn't. He wasn't mine to hug.

An elegantly manicured hand rested on his arm. The rage that had caused her to tremble just a few seconds ago was gone. Her shoulders had relaxed and her body was leaning toward him. Her voice was no longer loud enough to carry over the parking lot and I didn't hear what she said. I only saw the acceptance on Woods's face as he nodded. Her arm snaked around his and they walked inside the clubhouse together.

I opened my car door and tried hard not to think about the makeup sex they were probably going to have in his office. I couldn't think about it and remain calm. My attraction to

Woods was a door I needed to close. He was a friend only. The bitter taste in my mouth as I drove away and headed toward the condo only got stronger. I knew how it felt to be touched by Woods.

❧

A familiar Harley-Davidson was in the space beside mine. Tripp was here. I had to decide what I was going to do, and fast. Maybe he would ask me to leave. Maybe I wouldn't have a choice.

I made my way to the door of the condo and started to unlock it when I decided it was probably better to knock. I wasn't staying here alone anymore.

I knocked and waited.

Tripp opened the door almost right away, and his friendly smile turned into a frown. "You got a key. Why're you knocking?" he asked, stepping back and letting me in.

"Well, you're home now. I felt weird walking into your place without knocking," I replied. This was awkward. I needed to leave.

"Me coming home to visit doesn't change anything. You have a key, your stuff is here, you can come and go as you please. Don't let me being here bother you."

So he wanted me to stay? I hadn't expected that. Not really.

"I was thinking I might pack up and hit the road. I've made enough money to get me farther than Dallas this time."

Tripp tilted his head to the side and lowered his eyebrows as he studied me. "You leaving because I'm here?"

Yes. "No," I replied instead.

"Why don't I believe you?"

Because I was lying. I shrugged.

Tripp let out a sigh and closed the door. "Come on, blue eyes. You and I need to talk, and I want to do it while drinking a beer and looking at the gulf."

I followed him as we walked down the hall and into the kitchen. He stopped and grabbed two beers out of the fridge, then turned and tossed one to me. Luckily, I caught it. Tripp nodded toward the French doors leading out onto his balcony overlooking the water. I stepped outside first.

"Have a seat," Tripp said as he came up behind me. The warmth of his body was startling, and I quickly moved to sit down in one of the chairs set up around the patio table.

Tripp smirked at me as if he could read my mind and took a seat in the lounger, stretching his legs out in front of him and leaning back. "God, I've missed this place. Not the people in it but the place itself."

That was odd. Everyone I'd met missed Tripp. Did he just mean his parents, or did he truly not miss anyone here?

"You enjoying it here?" he asked, turning his head to look over at me.

"Yes. It's a nice place," I answered truthfully.

He grinned. "Yeah, it is."

"Why are you in Dallas then?" I asked. I'd heard from others why Tripp had left but I didn't know the whole story.

"My parents wanted me to be someone I wasn't. I wanted freedom. So I left. I couldn't be free here."

But he had come back.

"I won't be here long. The need to travel and experience life will get to me soon enough. I resigned at the bar. I'm positive Jeff is screwing the newest bartender. I can't keep working for that man. Besides, Dallas was getting old."

Was this his way of telling me I could stay? I wasn't sure

I wanted to. He didn't know me. I didn't know him, really. If I stayed here, he'd learn more about me than he probably wanted to know.

"I should be moving on along anyway. I've enjoyed staying in your place. It's really nice."

"Are we back to this again? I didn't come here to run you off. I don't want you to leave. At least not yet. You've only been here a few weeks. Enjoy the coast a little longer before you head out. I promise I'm a good roommate. I don't snore and I don't drink out of the milk carton unless it's almost empty and I'm finishing it off."

His teasing tone made me smile. It was time I was honest with him. I couldn't lie my way out of this one. He'd think I didn't like him, and I couldn't let him think that. Not after he'd been so kind to me.

"My leaving isn't because I'm worried you'll be a bad roommate," I began, and stopped. What did I say here? How did I explain this without sounding crazy?

"Good. Then there's no problem," he finished for me. That wasn't true, however.

"Yeah, there is. I'm the problem. I'm not exactly easy to live with. I . . . . I might not snore but I have bad dreams. They might . . . No, they will wake you up. I also have anxiety issues. I can hide it, but if we're living together then you're going to end up seeing me at my worst. I, I'm just not . . . Living with me isn't something anyone wants to do. Trust me. I need to just be on my way."

There, I'd said it. He could read between the lines.

Tripp sat up from his reclined position and put his feet on the ground. I watched as he leaned forward, resting his elbows on his knees and staring at me. I swallowed nervously. I didn't want to answer questions about this. If he made me remember too much then I'd show him exactly how insane I could be. I started to count sheep in my head. It helped fight off other thoughts.

"If that's the case then you don't need to be living alone anyway. How are you supposed to deal with that shit all by yourself? You're not." He paused and pressed his lips together tightly. I could tell he was choosing his next words with a great deal of care. "I've got my own demons. Ones that I keep tucked away. We're a pair, you and me. Both of us not ready to stay in one place and wanting to explore the world. I think we could be really good friends. It's why I gave you the keys to my place and sent you here. Who says we have to travel alone? I'm tired of being alone all the time. Why don't we let this be a trial run? We both stay here a couple of weeks and see if we can put up with the other one."

I let his words sink in. Responding to that was hard. I hadn't been expecting it and I wasn't sure what I thought about it. He wanted to travel around together? Didn't that seem intimate? We barely knew each other. But then, if we shared a condo for a few weeks, we'd know each other much better and he would be very sure that he couldn't deal with my crazy shit by then.

I wasn't going to overthink this. "Okay. Deal," I replied.

A slow smile spread across his face. That would all change really soon. Possibly tonight.

"Also, warning. Jace is happy I'm home. He's coming over tonight and he'll bring friends. I hope that's okay."

Things around here were about to get a lot more social. I needed to adjust.

Woods

A "Welcome Home, Tripp" party wasn't exactly something I wanted to attend. That was a shame, really. I liked Tripp. He was a friend. My bitterness over the fact that he was home and staying in his condo with Della was overriding everything else.

I was going so that I could get her alone and talk to her about this. I didn't want her to feel like she had to stay here if she was uncomfortable. I'd give her a fully furnished condo to stay in if she wanted it. She didn't have to stay with Tripp.

I knocked once, then walked on in. No one was going to be able to hear me over the noise anyway.

The place was packed. I scanned the crowd for Della.

"Woods, about damn time you showed up," Tripp called out over the music that was pumping through the condo's built-in speaker system. He was sitting at the bar with Jace, Bethy, Thad, and some unknown female who was sitting in Thad's lap. Della wasn't anywhere in the room. Dammit.

"And he's back," I said, forcing a smile.

"Just for a visit. Can't stay long. Dad will try and get a monkey suit on me if I do," he joked. But the words were too close for comfort. I knew what it felt like to have your father's claws imbedded deep.

"I'm trying to get him to stay. But he has it in his head he's only visiting before his next adventure," Jace said. I knew he was trying to ease my mind about Tripp being here. I could tell by his tone of voice. Right now, I just wanted to find Della.

"Where's Della?" I asked, unable to pretend like I wasn't here for her.

Tripp's eyebrows shot up and his gaze narrowed. I ignored it and looked directly at Jace.

Jace rolled his eyes and shook his head at me.

"She's in her room. Why?" Tripp replied.

"Why is she in her room? Is she okay?" I asked, looking back at the hall that led to the two bedrooms. Both doors were shut. Which one was she staying in?

"She had a phone call and went in there so she could hear. Again, why do you care?" Tripp asked.

I wasn't going to answer him. This wasn't his business. He was stopping through. He said so himself.

"Woods and Della met when she passed through a few months back. They uh . . . they uh . . . hooked up. They're friends now. He's a little protective," Jace explained.

"You're engaged," Tripp said, as if I needed reminding.

I leveled my gaze on him. "I wasn't when Della and I met. And it doesn't stop me from caring about her. I need to make sure she's okay," I said, before moving across the room toward the hallway.

I opened the first door and the lights were off. I closed that door and opened the next one. Della was sitting on the bed with her legs crossed and a phone pressed to her ear. Her eyes lifted to meet mine and they widened with surprise.

She was okay and I should close the door and walk away. But I didn't. I stepped inside and closed the door behind me.

"Uh, yeah. I need to go. I'll call you later," Della said into the phone as she watched me warily. "I'm fine. I just had company walk in and I don't want to be rude. Okay. Yeah. I love you, too. Bye."

She pressed the end button on her phone and slowly lowered it to her lap. "Woods?" The rest of her question was left open.

"You weren't out there." I nodded my head toward the door. "I wanted to check on you."

Understanding dawned on her face, and she gave me a small smile that made my chest feel tight. "Thank you, but you know you don't have to worry about me. I'm fine. Really I am."

She wasn't fine. I wasn't sure she'd ever been fine. I walked across the room and sat down beside her on the bed.

"I've wanted to come check on you since Friday night. You know you can call me if you ever need me."

She turned her head just an inch so she could meet my gaze. "You were busy with your fiancée this weekend. You don't have time to worry about me."

I had been with Angelina only today at lunch. "I've hardly seen Angelina this weekend," I replied, hating saying her name to Della. It seemed wrong.

Della dropped her eyes to stare down at her hands. "I saw the two of you when I got off work today." She didn't say more. I thought back to the disaster of a lunch we'd had with our parents and the fight we'd had on the ride over to the club. Then I'd apologized because Angelina had been right. I was torturing us both by being an ass.

"We had lunch together," I explained. I wasn't sure why I felt the need to explain, but I did.

"You fought and you made up. I don't understand how you can ever be happy, Woods." Her honest reply caused the tightness in my chest to ache.

112

"Me either."

"I can't let myself care about you anymore. I'm afraid of how I feel about you and I don't want to get hurt."

She was making it hard to breathe. The soft pleading in her voice was going to break me.

"I would never hurt you," I swore. I could never hurt her. I just wanted to protect her.

"But you do. Every time I see you with her it hurts. That's not your fault. It's mine. I cared too much too fast. And Friday night didn't help. It only made me care about you more."

We had barely even had a chance to be friends. She was already putting space between us. I couldn't let her do that. I needed her. She was the only bright spot in my life right now.

"What about our being friends?" I asked.

She shrugged and then squeezed her hands together tightly in her lap. "I don't know. I don't think I can. When you're . . . when you're sweet and caring like you were the other night . . . no one's ever been like that with me. At least not a guy. I can't seem to control my emotions."

Fuck. I couldn't lose this . . . this thing between us, but I also didn't want her hurt. I'd do anything to keep her from getting hurt.

"I want to be there for you when you need someone. Please don't push me away."

Della let out a sad laugh. "That's just it. You can't be there for me when I need someone. It makes my heart hurt just a little more each time. I'll be leaving soon. Let's just keep our distance until I go."

Hell no. I started to tell her just that when the door opened and Tripp stepped into the room.

"You okay?" he asked Della without looking my way. I didn't

like the way he looked at her. The concern in his eyes pissed me off.

"We were just talking about my leaving soon," she replied without looking up at him.

"You're not leaving," I argued. If she wanted to have this conversation in front of Tripp, then we'd fucking have it.

"I can't stay here," she replied.

"Yes you can."

"She doesn't want to, Woods. And why the urgency to get her to?" Tripp said, taking another step in Della's direction.

"Stay the fuck outta this conversation, Tripp. You don't know anything about her." Della stood and held up her hands to stop me from saying any more. "Stop it."

I looked up at her, and the sadness in her eyes tugged at me. I liked seeing them twinkling with laughter. Not like this.

"You need to step back and think about this bullshit you're doing. The Woods I remember wasn't an insensitive jerk. Della doesn't deserve this. You're engaged. Whatever you feel for Della has to end. She's leaving with me in a couple of weeks. We're going to travel together. Why don't you let this go, huh?"

She was leaving with him? The refusal to believe Della was going to leave with Tripp pounded in my head. Yet there she stood not denying it. Only looking sad and beaten down. Fuck this. I couldn't keep doing this to myself. She wasn't staying here. I had no future with Della. And if I didn't marry Angelina, I had no future in my father's company. Tripp's hand slipped over Della's shoulder and squeezed it. That was all I could handle. I stood up and stalked out of the room. I didn't look back. I didn't say good-bye to anyone. I just left.

Della

You shouldn't have told him that," I said without turning around and looking at Tripp. I shrugged his hand off my shoulder and walked over to the window. Woods had been so tormented. I could see the indecision on his face. I wanted him to choose me. But what would he be choosing? I wasn't a choice for anyone.

"He's engaged. He has no right coming in here and playing with your emotions like that. I saw the pain in your eyes. Whatever happened between the two of you is still there and he isn't letting it go. That's not fair to you."

Maybe it wasn't fair to me. But it wasn't fair to him, either. His choice had been made for him. He was unhappy and I hated that. I wanted to leave knowing he was happy.

"He's my friend," I replied. That was the only truth to all of this.

Tripp let out a heavy sigh. "Yeah, he's my friend, too. . . . Or he was. I think he's considering murdering me the first chance he gets. But he could leave this behind. He could have chosen you."

"I'm not a choice," I replied.

My words were followed by silence. I stood there looking out over the ocean. I could feel Tripp's gaze still on me. He was thinking about my words. I wouldn't explain them. He'd understand them soon enough.

"Not everyone sees you the way you do. Sometimes our imperfections are what make us special."

I didn't reply. Because he was right—that was the case with many people. However, not with me. It wasn't my imperfections I was worried about. It was the terror that twisted everything in my life and kept me apart from everyone else.

The door softly closed behind me. He was leaving me alone. Good. I wanted to be alone.

"Do you know why I sent you here?" Tripp's voice startled me and I spun around. He was sitting on the edge of the bed. He hadn't left.

I shook my head. I had no idea why he'd sent me. We'd barely known each other.

"Because you looked as lost as I felt. I had been watching you for weeks. It's hard not to watch you." A crooked smile tugged at his lips. "And you didn't seem to know where you belonged. Neither do I. Since I left this world behind I've just been drifting. I'm tired of being alone. I saw a kindred spirit in you and I sent you here to keep you until I had the guts to come back and face this place." He paused and ran a hand through his hair. "I planned on spending time with you and getting to know you better. But this isn't exactly something I was prepared for. Woods." He shook his head. "You had to go and get mixed up with Woods. Of all people. Someone just as screwed up as I once was. Problem is, he isn't going to run. He wants this shitty life our parents forced on us. He is becoming a motherfucking puppet. You can do better than that, Della."

I swallowed the nervous knot lodged in my throat. I wasn't sure what all Tripp planned on saying, but I didn't want to

116

hear any more. He was right. Woods wasn't someone I needed to waste my time wanting. But forgetting him and moving on was easier said than done.

"Tonight I just need to go to sleep. I don't have my sights set on Woods if that's what you're thinking. We had sex. That's all there is between us."

Tripp stood up. "I'm sorry about tonight."

I was, too. I was sorry about a lot of things. "It's okay. I'm just tired."

Trip nodded once, then left the room.

I sank down on the bed and covered my face with my hands. I was more lost now than I had been three weeks ago.

"Were you outside, Della? How could you? What do I have to do to get it through your head that you can't go outside? It's dangerous out there." The shrill screech of my mother's voice was nothing like the searing pain from the leather belt that she slashed across my legs. I knew not to cry out in pain. She'd only get angrier. My sneaking out of the house always sent her into a tailspin.

My knees buckled as the tender skin behind them tore open from the continuous hit of the leather.

"Diseases. There are diseases out there that you could bring into this house. You're not only being reckless, you're being self-ish," she yelled, and I was thankful that it muffled the sound of my cries. I wasn't able to hold back anymore. The pain was too much. Sometimes I wondered why I even came back after I sneaked out. Why didn't I run? Keep running until I was free of this. Of her.

But I couldn't. She needed me. I would never be free. I couldn't leave her. She was my mother. She was all I had.

117

"Do you think of me? NO! Do you think of your brother? NO! This upsets him, you leaving the house. How could you?" she yelled as another slash sliced open the backs of my legs. I would start wishing I was the child that was dead when the beatings were this bad. The pain was too much.

The scene changed and my mother was no longer looming over me with her crazed, fearful face as she beat me. Instead there was no life in her eyes as she lay in a pool of blood. I started to scream.

"Shhhh, Della, it's okay. I've got you. Shhhh." The voice was far away but I heard it. The images of my mother's death slowly faded as I focused more on the voice. The sobs were mine. I recognized them.

"That's it. You're okay. I'm here," the voice said gently.

I opened my eyes, and as they came into focus, I realized the voice was Tripp's. The fear on his face said enough. He was holding me in his arms as he rocked me back and forth saying soothing words. He hadn't been prepared for what he'd just seen. I could see the questions in his eyes.

"I'm sorry," I managed to croak out. My throat was raw from the screaming. It always was when I woke up like this. Braden had been the first person ever to experience this with me. My psychologist had said it was a night terror. That my trauma was being expressed while I was asleep and my guard was down. Unfortunately, nothing I'd done had helped this. When I slept, my mother always came. Then the memories came with her.

"Hush," he said, putting his finger over my mouth and shaking his head. "Don't. I can't deal with you apologizing right now."

I didn't say anything more. I moved out of his lap and back over to the side of the bed I slept on. Tripp didn't move. He stayed where he was.

"Do you do that often?" he finally asked.

"Yes," I replied. Because it happened most nights. But normally I woke up on my own once the images of that night when I'd found my mother came back to me.

"And you deal with that alone, every night?" he asked.

I nodded.

"Fuck," he whispered, and stood up. "Della, why are you alone? You shouldn't be alone! How the hell have you managed this long?" He rubbed his palms over his eyes and then ran his hands over his hair in a frustrated gesture. "That was intense. Do you even know how scary that shit is? God, Della, you can't stay alone."

I pulled the covers up to my chin and leaned against the headboard. This was where Tripp realized traveling with me was much more than he had bargained for. It had been only a matter of time.

"I'm fine. Someone being with me doesn't make the dreams go away. I have them anyway. I'll leave in the morning."

Tripp shook his head and walked over to sit down in front of me. "You aren't going anywhere in the morning. Whatever is running through your head, you're wrong. This isn't a deal breaker for me, Della. I just wasn't prepared for it."

I wasn't sure I believed him, but I nodded anyway.

"In the morning I'm taking you golfing. Then we're going to have lunch together. It's time the two of us got to know each other better."

Woods

I hadn't been able to sleep. I'd sat out on my balcony all night and stared at the waves while I faced several facts. The first one I finally accepted was that I would never be happy being married to Angelina and neither would she. The second one was that I was going to have to let go of my dream of taking over Kerrington Club one day. My dad wasn't going to forgive me for not doing his bidding and marrying a Greystone. Della had changed everything. I just didn't give a shit anymore. I wanted her. Maybe it wasn't forever, but for whatever length of time I had with her, I wanted her. I couldn't keep thinking about her and torturing myself with the idea of not getting to have her.

My future was about to be completely thrown off track because Della Sloane was under my skin and I had to have her. I couldn't ignore it anymore. It wasn't just the sex. It had been in the beginning, but not now. I'd gotten close enough to her to see deeper. I knew she was selfless and thoughtful. She didn't expect anything from me and was just happy to be alive. She was wounded but still fought hard to make it past that. No sob story. It was all part of her beautiful package. Had I ever known a girl like that?

The relief that came with the acceptance that I wasn't going to give up something that could be the best thing I'd ever found in order to fulfill my father's orders was incredible. I could take a deep breath with ease.

I picked up my phone and asked Angelina to meet me in my office at eleven. That would give her time to sleep in and get dressed. Then after that was over, I was going to find Della and get on my knees and beg if I had to.

Leaving her with Tripp last night had been the slap in my face I needed. This farce of a relationship I had with Angelina was ridiculous. She knew it, too. We were both so power hungry to take the places that were rightfully ours in our fathers' businesses that we were willing to forgo love. Even if Della hadn't walked into my life and forced me to walk away from my dad's demands, I wouldn't have been able to walk down the aisle and say "I do."

⊥

The swift knock on my office door came before Angelina opened it and stepped inside. Her long blond hair was pulled up in a twist with curls cascading loose from the top. Her short purple linen dress was without a wrinkle, and I was willing to bet her matching heels cost more than the average person made in six months. The diamond ring on her left hand mocked me as the sunlight pouring in through the window reflected off it and danced around the room. It was as perfectly polished and set as the woman's hand it adorned. Angelina had always been beautiful and elegant. She'd been raised to be her father's pawn. The young girl I'd once cared for was somewhere underneath all that facade.

"Don't do this," she said, stiffening her spine and reaching out to grasp the back of the chair beside her. I hadn't said a word but she already knew. That should have been confirmation enough for both of us.

"We can't do what they want us to. I let him force my hand this far, but I'm done. I can't."

Angelina's eyes flashed with anger and disgust. She didn't understand. I'd thought maybe she would thank me but I could see that wouldn't be happening. She had been prepared to go through with this. Why? Her father would find someone else. Possibly someone who could love her. Who wouldn't just be marrying her for her father's name and fortune.

"You're making the biggest mistake of your life," she said through clenched teeth.

I walked over to the other side of my desk and sat down.

"Marrying you would have been the biggest mistake of my life. We would have hated each other. I can't let my father keep controlling me. If he doesn't want me to have this business, then fine. At least I will have made my own decisions."

Angelina rolled her eyes as if what I was saying was ridiculous. "Listen to yourself. This world is all you've ever known. This life you are so willing to toss away because you don't want to be told what to do, is *all you've known*. You're acting as if marrying me is the worst possible thing you could ever do. We were close once, Woods. We were friends. We could have that again if you would just accept this and be open to it."

We had been two kids whose parents had left us alone all the time. We'd shared the same screwed-up life. She was right; we'd been friends. But I'd never wanted anything more.

"Because we were friends once, I refuse to let us both be forced into something we didn't choose. You have never been given another choice. Since we were kids your parents shoved me down your throat. There is someone out there that will love you. They'll want you for you. Don't settle for less. Life is short and I'm tired of wasting it."

She threw her hands up and let out an aggravated growl. "Fine. Whatever. I'm not begging you. It isn't like I can't do better. I just figured marrying you would be the best for me. You know me and we have a history. But I won't keep this up. I have pride and I won't stand here and beg." She slipped the diamond off her finger and slammed it down on the edge of my desk. "Take it. We both know I don't need it."

I started to say something more. Apologize, or at least try and ease her mind, but there was nothing else I could say. I needed to count myself lucky that she hadn't hurled anything at my head.

"Good-bye, Woods. I hope this was worth it to you," she spat, then stalked out of my office.

I waited until she'd had time to get out of the building before I left. I had to go find Della.

Della

I sucked at golf.

When the ball once again went flying out into the trees, I spun around and looked at Tripp, who was covering his mouth to smother his laughter. At least he found my extreme lack of luck with a golf swing humorous.

When he had woken me up at seven this morning to make the tee time he'd reserved, I hadn't been very happy. But after the way he'd helped me get through my episode the night before, I felt like I owed it to him. So I had dragged myself out of bed and gotten dressed. Now, seventeen holes and twelve lost balls later, I was thinking I should have stayed in bed. Yes, I'd wanted to learn to golf, but not this early, and now that I knew I was terrible at it, I didn't want to try again.

"I give up," I said, handing him the club.

"You're getting better. You just jacked this one up," Tripp said with a chuckle.

"Save it. We both know I'm horrible at this. Can I just watch you play out the rest?"

Tripp slid the club back into the bag. "We can call it a game. You tried hard. Maybe we need to spend a little time on the driving range and work on your swing before we attempt this again."

He was talking like we'd be golfing together in the future.

I didn't want to ever golf again if I could help it. I didn't want to sound rude, so I just kept my mouth shut. I got on the golf cart, and Tripp drove us back to the clubhouse.

Without thinking about it, I started looking for Woods's truck. I could tell myself it was because I wanted to make sure he wasn't here and I wouldn't have to see him. But I'd be lying. I was a glutton for punishment.

"Dammit," Tripp muttered before pulling the golf cart into the first empty spot reserved for the carts.

I glanced over at him to see what was wrong, when my gaze locked on Woods. He was headed toward us.

"He looks like a man on a mission," Tripp said in a low voice, then stepped out of the cart. Woods nodded at Tripp, but his eyes immediately were back on me. I watched as he walked past Tripp.

He stopped in front of me. "We need to talk," he said.

"Y'all did enough of that last night, man." Tripp's tone sounded like a gentle warning.

Woods ignored him. "I'm not engaged anymore. Angelina just left and it's over. I ended it." He reached out and slipped his hand into mine. "Please come talk to me."

He'd broken off his engagement? I felt like I was still sleeping. Why would he do that? He wanted what a marriage to Angelina would give him. Why had he ended that?

"I don't understand," I replied. My voice was barely above a whisper.

A sexy grin tilted the corners of Woods's mouth. "That's why we need to talk."

I glanced over at Tripp, who just shrugged. I had lunch plans with him today. I couldn't cancel on him. I needed him to say something instead of just shrugging at me.

"We . . . Tripp and I were supposed to have lunch together," I said, still looking at Tripp.

Tripp looked from me to Woods, then he shook his head with a small smile. "I'm not getting in the middle of this. Go with him. If he just broke it off with Angelina, then there's more to what he's got to say than I thought there was." His complete attention went to Woods. "No one's puppet. It's about damn time," he said, then walked off.

Woods was grinning when I looked back at him. "Have lunch with me?"

I glanced past him toward the club's restaurant. I didn't want to go in there with the boss and have lunch. I couldn't let one of my coworkers wait on me. But I also wanted to talk to Woods. He wasn't engaged. My heart started beating harder in my chest. Woods was free.

"I wouldn't be comfortable eating in there. Could we talk first, then go find something to eat somewhere else?"

"Whatever you want." He pulled me to him and then nodded toward his truck. "Let's go for a ride."

Once we were in the truck, Woods didn't start the engine. He looked over at me. His dark brown eyes were serious, but the sadness wasn't there. "I'm sorry for how I acted last night. I shouldn't have talked to you that way. I was panicking and I lost it."

I shifted in my seat and rested my shoulder against the leather so that I was facing him. "Why were you panicking?"

Woods cocked one eyebrow as if he didn't think this question needed an answer. As if it was understood. "Because Tripp was talking about taking you away."

Oh.

"I want you to understand something. This needs to be

very clear. I never loved Angelina. I never wanted to be engaged to her. I was doing it because she was the key to getting what I thought I'd always wanted. But you changed that. I realized I wanted other things. I didn't want to be controlled. And I wanted a chance with you. Even if you don't plan on staying long. Even if you aren't one for commitments, I want this time with you."

The idea of losing his freedom hadn't been enough reason for him to refuse to do his father's bidding? It had taken me to make him stand up to his father? Why me? I didn't understand. "What if you get to know me and you realize I'm not worth it? Will you still be glad you let go of everything?"

Woods's grin returned and he nodded. "Yeah. Like Tripp said out there. I'm no one's puppet. It was time I put my foot down."

He was right. Living under someone else's control wasn't living at all. I knew that all too well. But I didn't want to be the only reason he gave up what was rightfully his. The pressure to be worth it was too much.

"I agree. Not being able to make your own choices in life isn't fair. I guess I just want to be sure I'm not the reason you did this. Because honestly, you're gonna find out real soon that I'm more of a mess than you already got a glimpse of the other night."

Woods's eyebrows lowered as he frowned at me. He didn't like me saying that, but he didn't know the truth about me. I wasn't going to tell him, either.

"I don't like to hear you talk about yourself like that," he said in a husky voice.

I turned my body back around in my seat. "We can discuss that another time. I'm starving." I wanted to ask him more questions—like, What happens with your job now? or Will your dad fire you? or Do you have plans to do something else?—but I was refusing to talk anymore about me and my future, so I couldn't expect him to open up about his.

We could go eat and just see what happened next. He might realize what he'd done before the day was through and go running back to Angelina begging her to forgive him. There was no need for deep conversations right now. I just wanted to enjoy spending time with him and not feel guilty about wanting a taken man.

Woods

Della had eaten her sandwich in silence. She'd been rather focused on her food since it arrived at the table. I'd had a hard time eating because watching her was more entertaining. She patted her mouth with a napkin and her eyes lifted to meet mine. A blush tinted her cheeks and her eyes twinkled.

"I was starving. Golf exhausted me and I'm not sure why because I was terrible at it," she explained as she lowered the napkin to her lap.

"Was today your first time playing golf?" I asked, trying to push back my immediate jealous reaction to the fact Tripp had taken her golfing today.

"Yes. I wanted to learn to play and Tripp wanted me to go with him today so I went. But I think I lost so many of his golf balls he regrets it."

This time I laughed. I knew Tripp didn't regret a single minute of it. I just hoped he had enough memories to hold him for the rest of his damn life, because that was his only chance to get her alone like that. "You just need a good instructor," I replied.

Della pinched her lips in a thoughtful frown. Then she shook her head. "No, I'm hopeless. I wouldn't plan on wasting your time."

The chance to get to wrap my arms around her and teach her to swing a club, then stand back and watch her ass while she did it was not a waste of time. I kept that thought to myself, though.

"We'll see" was all I said.

The waitress brought us our ticket, and I slipped onto the table enough cash to cover the meal and a decent tip before standing up and holding my hand out to Della. I was tired of being in public with her. I wanted to get her alone. There was a lot I wanted to say, but first I needed to hold her. It had been too long.

"Where are we going now?" she asked as she stood up beside me.

"My place. I want you to see it. Especially the view. Is that okay?"

Della nodded, and I tried to be good. It was hard though. The image of her naked against my sheets wouldn't go away. I wanted her there.

"I'd love to see your place."

We walked back outside to my truck. Della climbed up in the passenger seat and I didn't even pretend like I wasn't checking out her ass in the little white shorts she was wearing. There wasn't a panty line, and the idea of her not having on anything underneath made me break out into a sweat. I needed to think about something else, anything else, or I was going to be hard as a rock and incredibly uncomfortable.

"How long is Tripp in town?" There, that should do it. Remind myself she was sharing a condo with another man. One who no doubt wanted her, too.

"He didn't say exactly. I think he was just ready to move on from Dallas and came back here before his next adventure."

The way she talked about Tripp's life like it made complete sense reminded me that she led a life much like his. One I didn't understand. But then, if my dad fired me, I would be just as lost as he was. Leaving town with Della didn't sound like such a bad idea.

My phone rang in my pocket and I knew without answering it was my father. It had taken Angelina longer than I expected to get word to him that the engagement was over. His grand plan was ruined.

I reached into my pocket and turned the phone off. I would deal with him later. Right now I wanted to focus on Della. Facing my father was going to put a major damper on my mood. I didn't want that today.

"Do you work tonight?" I asked. Because if she did, I was going to call in and change the schedule.

"This is my day off," she replied, grinning. "Don't you do the scheduling?"

I did, but this past week had been hell. I couldn't remember what day I'd given her off. "Just checking," I replied before pulling into the split-brick drive that led up to my house. It had been my parents' first home. My grandfather had let them live here until my father earned enough to buy them the house my mother really wanted. When my grandfather passed away, he'd left the house to me. Even something that small had pissed my father off. He'd wanted complete control over me. What I'd really needed my grandfather to leave me was a part of the club. He hadn't.

"Woods! It's beautiful," Della said in awe as I pulled underneath the raised house. It wasn't really. Not compared to my parents' or most of the newer homes in Rosemary. But it had character.

"Thank you."

Della opened the truck door and hopped out before I could help her.

"It's like one of those seaside houses you see in the movies. The big hurricane shutters and the wraparound porch. This is just perfect."

Hearing her gush about my house made me want to haul her upstairs to my room even more. I loved this place. It was the only thing that was mine.

"I can't wait to see the inside. I could just live on your porch. The view must be perfect."

She could live on my porch if she wanted. I'd even let her come inside and sleep in my bed. I didn't say that though. Too much, too soon. Right now we'd had a few shared moments and some hot sex. I had to build on that. I wanted to build on that.

"Come on up. I'll show you just how perfect the view is."

Della followed me up the stairs, and I unlocked the door, then stood back and let her walk inside first. I hadn't given much thought to my decorating before, but knowing Della was here and checking everything out, I hated the fact that I'd not changed much since my grandfather left me the house.

My grandmother had decorated it, and they'd lived here the last few years of my grandmother's life. When she'd been diagnosed with terminal cancer, they sold their sprawling mansion in Seaside and moved back here. After she'd passed away my grandfather moved into my parents' house and lived there for three months before he died of a heart attack.

I liked the warmth of the place. I hadn't spent much time thinking of changing things. It wasn't like I entertained here. I worked too much for that lifestyle.

Della ran her hand along the worn pale leather couch and

spun around slowly, looking at the details my grandmother had taken great care to leave behind. She had loved to paint. Seeing the canvases she'd painted out on that porch while she enjoyed the last years she had on earth always gave me a sense of peace.

"The paintings are beautiful. So bright and cheerful," Della said as she stood in front of one that was my grandfather's favorite. When I'd tried to give it to him he'd refused to take it. He'd said she wanted it here in this place.

"That's a hole at the golf course," she said. I was impressed that she recognized it.

"My grandfather's favorite. His only hole in one was at that hole. It's the fifteenth."

Della smiled. "And you have it here on your wall."

"My grandmother painted it. She painted all of these."

Della's eyes went wide and she started looking around at the other paintings on the wall. "She was very talented."

I had to agree. She was. Yet she'd given up her dreams for my grandfather's. I'd always heard my mother's bitter comments about her not being the doormat that my grandmother was. But I never saw my grandmother as a doormat. She was quiet and reserved, but she'd controlled so much more than anyone understood. She had owned my grandfather's heart. As cold and unfeeling as many assumed it was, she had owned it. And she'd cherished it.

"It's not what I expected . . . not from a single guy," she said in almost a whisper. "I love it."

"Come see the view," I said, opening the doors leading out onto the porch. Della walked out and went straight to the railing. The ocean breeze caught her hair and it danced around her shoulders. I liked seeing her out here. I stepped back inside and went to grab a bottle of wine and two glasses.

Della

Here," Woods said, walking up behind me.

I turned to look at him and saw he was holding a glass of red wine. I took it and hoped my inexperience in the red wine department wasn't too apparent on my face when I took a sip. I was positive this was expensive, but I wouldn't have been able to tell the difference between cheap and good wine. I'd had very little.

"Thank you," I managed to reply without sounding as unsure as I felt.

"Come sit down. We can see the view just as good from over here," he said, nodding toward two teak lounge chairs.

I walked over and sank down on the thick quilted cushion and stretched my legs out in front of me.

With his leg, Woods scooted the lounger beside me closer, then lowered himself down onto it. He moved the armrest that separated us. If I shifted even an inch I would brush up against him. It was tempting.

"I didn't ask if you liked red wine," he said.

He was probably noticing my small sips. I was deciding that I did like it. I wasn't sure how it would affect me though.

"I wasn't positive I liked it or not. I've not really had much of it in the past. But this is good."

He smirked and took a drink. I really shouldn't have stared at him, but the muscles in his throat moved as he swallowed and it was mesmerizing. Woods set his glass down on the table on the other side of his chair but he didn't take his eyes off me.

"I'd planned to be good tonight. But I can't. Not with you looking at me like that," Woods said as he took the glass from my hand and put it down beside his. "I think I'll be okay if I can just have a little. Just a small taste. It's been too long and I can't seem to think about anything other than how much I want to kiss you"—he brushed his finger over my lips—"and the many parts of you I want to touch," he said, slipping one of his hands around my waist. Then his hand slid down farther until it was cupping my butt. "Fuck, baby, you aren't wearing any panties under these shorts."

The reminder of the thin fabric being the only barrier down there to soak up the moisture his words were causing concerned me. I did not want a damp spot on my shorts. That would be humiliating.

"Come here," he ordered, picking me up by the waist and pulling me onto his lap. I didn't want to straddle him. What if I was already wet down there? His hand closed over my thigh and I shivered, unable to stop him from moving my leg over his lap until my crotch was hovering over him. I was going to ruin these shorts.

Woods's hands slipped into my hair and pulled my head down until his lips covered mine. The moment his tongue eased into my mouth and flicked against mine, I no longer cared about the possible shorts fiasco I might have to deal with later. I just wanted more of him. He cupped my face with one hand and then ran the tip of his very talented tongue over the roof of my mouth, causing me to sink down onto him. The hard ridge of his erection pressed firmly against the burning ache that was alive and ready. I knew how good Woods felt inside me, and my body was screaming for more.

"So sweet," he murmured against my lips. Then his attentive mouth began to tease my jawline until his open mouth pressed against my neck. The heat from his breath made my nipples throb.

Woods moved his hand between my legs until he found the evidence of my arousal. "Already wet," he said against my neck, then suckled the skin there gently. "Do you know how incredibly sexy it is that your shorts are wet?" I didn't respond. I couldn't. I was holding my breath in anticipation. "I don't think you do," he said, continuing to kiss down my neck.

"Della, tonight wasn't supposed to be about sex," he said, looking up at me through lowered lashes. His mouth was so close to my cleavage, I wanted to shove my chest in his face and beg. "I just needed a taste. Trouble is, I forgot how intoxicating you smell. I want inside you, baby. Right here. I want to rip these shorts off your body and slide deep inside you." I was ready to agree to anything if he'd just touch me some more. A small whimper escaped me, and I didn't even care that I was showing him how weak and needy I was.

"Are you hurting?" he asked as he reached up and tugged the front of my shirt down, and then my bra, until both my breasts were free. "I'm a tit man and these titties are like fucking nirvana. So round and soft." He pressed a kiss to one of my pebbled-up nipples and then stuck his tongue out and ran it slowly over the tip. "Perfect little round cherries. Meant to be sucked on," he whispered before pulling it into his mouth and doing just that. I couldn't keep myself from grabbing his head desperately and holding him there. I didn't want him to stop.

I could feel it all the way down between my legs. Each tug of my nipple had delicious waves of pleasure rolling through me. Woods's hand slipped into the front of my shorts and I lifted my hips to give him better access. He covered my smooth mound and groaned when his finger found my slick heat. I was soaked, and any other time I would care. Right now I just needed more.

Two of his fingers found my swollen clit and began to rub it in a steady rhythm matching the sucking his mouth was doing on my nipple. He pulled his head back and moved to the other breast. That was as far as I was letting his head move away.

The magic that only Woods seemed to be able to cause started to build and I spread my thighs wider. He pinched down on my clit at the same time he bit my nipple, and the bliss I had been expecting exploded around me. I pulled his hair and screamed his name while my whole body shook from the violent orgasm.

"Ah, God," he gasped, and wrapped his arms around my body, holding me against his chest. I collapsed against him. Woods's breathing was as heavy as my own, and I let go of the handfuls of his hair I still had in my grasp.

"I'm sorry," I managed to croak out.

"For what?" Woods asked with his mouth pressed against my neck.

"Pulling your hair."

A soft chuckle vibrated his body, and he licked at the tender flesh he'd nibbled on earlier. "Don't be. That was hot. So fucking hot. Anytime you want to pull my hair while you're screaming my name, go right ahead."

I felt his erection jerk underneath me, and my throbbing well-pleased body jumped in response. We weren't finished.

That had just been an appetizer. I rocked my hips against him, savoring the pleasant pain it created. Woods's hands clamped down on my hips and held me still. "Don't."

I froze. Was I hurting him?

He sucked in a breath, then picked me up and eased me off him. Maybe I had been too loud out here and he was going to move us inside.

"I've got some work to do. I should take you home."

What? Home? Huh? I sat there as he stood up and adjusted himself. I didn't move to follow him. I was still processing what was happening.

He glanced down at me, and what looked like a wince crossed his face. Before I could ask what was wrong, he reached down to pull my bra and shirt back into place, then took my hand and pulled me up.

"I have to take you back" was all he said before grabbing the wineglasses and walking inside.

Like someone on autopilot, I followed him. He put both our glasses on his bar and then grabbed his keys. He glanced back at me and smiled, then nodded toward the door.

We were really leaving. Okay. My stomach felt sick. I'd done something wrong. Had he seen how much I craved his touch? Did that scare him? It scared me that I wanted him to touch me so badly. It scared me that he made me feel comfort in ways no one else had ever been able to. I was willing to do anything to make him want to be close to me longer. Going back to the condo only meant another night ahead with dreams I wanted to escape. Memories that controlled me. I wanted what Woods could give me. But that wouldn't happen. He was getting rid of me.

Woods

Once I got her safely in my truck, I planned on explaining. The confusion in her big blue eyes had been obvious. But every time I tried to, I couldn't think of a way to say it without scaring her off.

I was also afraid she might argue with me, and all it was going to take to get me to snap was one little pleading look from her. My cock was still throbbing painfully, and the fact that I knew she wasn't wearing any damn panties and she was soaking wet from that orgasm I'd given her was only making me harder.

Throwing her on my bed and fucking her until I had her screaming my name again and telling me that her tight little pussy was mine had been the only thing I could think about while I touched her.

But then she'd gone off in my lap, and I knew this was my moment to prove to me and her that I could be selfless. Tonight had been about her. Not what she could do for me but just about her pleasure. I didn't want this relationship to be built on sex. There was more there with Della. I liked being around her. I wanted to protect her. She had me so wrapped up I couldn't think clearly.

Taking her back to Tripp's *motherfucking* condo was going

to kill me. I didn't want her sleeping there with him in the next room, but I couldn't exactly move her into my place, either. That was moving way too fast, and a girl like Della would run. I didn't want her to run. I'd chase her ass down if she tried, but I still didn't want her to try. I wanted her to stay because she wanted to be with me.

Being the kind of guy a girl stayed for was harder than I thought.

"Did I do something wrong?" Della asked, breaking into my thoughts. I was already pulling up to Tripp's condo. I'd been so torn about what to say to her that I hadn't said anything. Shit. She was worried. I parked the truck and looked over at her. The frown creasing her forehead bothered me. I didn't mean to make her frown.

I reached over and soothed the puckered skin with my thumb. "No, not at all. You were perfect."

Her frown didn't go away. She wasn't buying it. I should have explained this to her. I just couldn't find the right words.

"Okay. If you're sure," she said slowly, and reached for the door handle.

"Wait, I got it. I'll walk you to the door," I said, jerking my door open and going around to open her door. She watched me, still frowning with a confused look on her face. It was adorable. I took her hands and helped her down. My eyes zeroed in on the very visible wet spot on the crotch of her shorts. Glancing around, I looked for Tripp's Harley and found it sitting over by Della's car. Hell no. He wasn't seeing this. Evidence of her wet pussy was for my eyes only. Reaching into the truck, I grabbed a hoodie out of the backseat.

"Wear this," I said, pulling it over her head before she could protest or even ask why. She obediently put her hands into the

140

arms and it fell to the middle of her thighs. Completely covering her and her shorts. I let out a sigh of relief.

"Why am I wearing your sweatshirt?" she asked, studying me like she thought I might be going crazy.

I slipped my hand around her waist and pulled her closer to me, then lowered my head until my mouth was at her ear. "Tripp's home, and that sweet little wet spot on those shorts of yours is for no one's eyes but mine. When you get inside, go change into something loose and baggy. And for all that's holy, please wear panties and a bra."

Della nodded, and I let her go and stepped back. She smelled too good. Seeing her dwarfed in my hoodie wasn't helping. It was making my swollen dick even worse. "Go on inside. I need to stay here. If I go to the door I won't be able to leave."

She stuck her hands into the front pockets of the hoodie. "Okay. I'll, uh, I'll see you tomorrow then," she stammered, then turned and walked to the condo. I waited until she was safely inside before I got back in my truck and left. I should have walked her to the door, but I knew seeing her in Tripp's apartment would bring out the caveman in me even more and I would follow her inside and go lock us both in her room. This had been the only way to let her go.

It was time I went and dealt with my dad.

My mother met me at the door with a frown. She didn't ask how I was doing or even attempt small talk. She just pointed down the hall and said, "Your dad's in his office." Then she walked away without another word.

Most of my life my mother was affectionate only if I was

doing exactly what she wanted me to. Whenever I failed or displeased her, she let me know exactly how she felt about me. I should have been over it by now. I was a twenty-four-year-old man. Seeking my mother's approval was a thing of my past. Still, her conditional love was hard to swallow at times.

I knocked on the door to my father's office, then opened it up. No use in waiting on him to tell me to come in. He was mad at me anyway. He was sitting at his desk with the phone to his ear when I walked inside. His eyes glared at me with disapproval through his reading glasses.

"Of course. I agree. Woods has just walked into my office. I'll speak with him and get back to you on where we go from here," he said into the phone before hanging it up and leaning back in his chair to study me with a look of disdain.

The bitterness I felt from the knowledge that my grandfather had given him the title of vice president and moved him into the big office the year he graduated from college was always there. He acted like I had to prove so much to him when I'd worked more in that club than he had. He had never gotten his hands dirty or dealt with employees. Yet he expected me to pay my dues.

"I hope you're here to explain to me why you would toss away everything we've worked for because you think *you'll be unhappy*. That's bullshit, son. No red-blooded man would be unhappy with a woman like Angelina Greystone."

He hadn't worked for anything. He wasn't being told whom he had to marry. I gritted my teeth and held the curses and insults in. They wouldn't help matters now.

"I don't love her. She doesn't even like me much. I couldn't go through with it. I'm sorry but as much as I want the job I was raised believing would be mine, I won't ruin my life and hers."

My father leaned forward and rested his elbows on his desk. "Love doesn't make a good marriage. It isn't forever. It leaves you. When reality sets in and times get hard, the love disappears and you're left with nothing. You marry someone who wants the same things you do. Who isn't expecting romance but success. Angelina gets this. You don't."

When my grandmother was sick, I went to visit my grandparents every chance I got. One day I was sitting on the porch with my grandfather as he watched my grandmother paint one of her many pictures. The love and affection on his face were unmistakable. He'd turned to me that day and said, "Don't miss out on the love of a good woman, son. No matter what that old man of yours tells you, love is real. I'd have never had the success in my life without that woman right there. She's been my backbone. She's been my reason for everything I've ever done. One day your drive to make a name for yourself will begin to drift away. It won't be that important anymore. But when you're doing it for someone else, someone you would move heaven and earth for, then you never lose the desire to succeed. I can't imagine this world without her in it. I don't even want to."

I hadn't thought about those words again until today. The man who had raised my father was similar to him in many ways. But there was a difference. My dad did all this for himself. His drive to succeed was selfish. There was no love in his work. My grandfather had built this business out of love for the woman he married. I'd seen that with my own eyes. I didn't want to be my father. I wanted to be my grandfather.

"We need to agree to disagree," I finally said, knowing the mention of his parents would only infuriate him. He'd always thought my grandfather had made bad decisions even though he was the man who built this club.

143

My father smirked and shook his head. "No, son, we don't, because I'm in charge here. If you're choosing not to do what is best for this club and your future, then you're not ready to take over anything. I can't promote you if I can't trust you to make smart decisions. Your job at the club is safe for now, but that doesn't mean someone I can trust more to do your job won't come along."

Not only was he not going to give me the position I'd worked hard for but he was threatening the position I currently had. I wanted to tell him to fuck himself and walk out. Before this was over I might end up doing just that. However, out of respect for the man who'd built this with the desire to hand it down to each generation of the Kerrington name, I would stay. That man I respected. The one in front of me I held no respect for. If he pushed me too far, I'd be gone. I wondered if he'd even miss me then.

Della

I changed into sweats and a T-shirt before walking back into the living room and talking to Tripp. I preferred to stay in this room and think about everything. I was still trying to figure out what happened and what I did wrong with Woods. He was giving me all kinds of mixed signals. Either he was disgusted by me and decided not to have sex with me or he had just been ready to get rid of me. I wasn't sure. But then he'd made me wear his shirt and told me to change into baggy clothes. I didn't know what to think about that.

As soon as I'd had that orgasm in his lap, he'd been ready to get me the hell away from him. On the drive over here I had convinced myself that I'd screamed too loud and hurt him by pulling his hair like a crazed woman. Then maybe he was as embarrassed by the wet spot on my shorts as I was and that's why he covered me up. He didn't want Tripp to see me and know he'd been the cause of that. I reached over, picked his hoodie back up, and pulled it over my head. It smelled like Woods. I liked that. I had wanted to get to smell more of him tonight. The feeling of rejection I'd hoped to avoid was settling in.

I could talk to Tripp. I wouldn't tell him exactly what happened, but I could get his guy opinion on things.

Tripp's eyes lifted from the book he was reading and he

145

smiled up at me. "Already wearing Kerrington's clothes. Damn, the guy moves fast," he teased.

I sighed and sank down on the sofa across from the chair he was sitting in. "Not what it looks like. Trust me." The deflation in my voice was a little more obvious than I intended.

"Uh-oh. What's wrong?" Tripp asked, setting his book down on the table beside him and sitting up straighter.

I thought about my words carefully. I didn't want to tell him too much, but I did want his opinion. "Woods broke things off with Angelina and we went to talk about that," I began. Tripp nodded. He already knew this much, but I was still scrambling to figure out what to say to him. "We had lunch together and he explained that he wasn't happy with her. He doesn't want to be told who to marry. Then we went back to his place. He wanted to show me his house and I loved it." I paused and chewed on my bottom lip a moment to think about my next words.

"He never takes girls to that house. It was his grandparents', so it's his off-limits place. I've only been there a handful of times."

That caught my attention. "His grandmother's paintings are still all over the walls. They're beautiful."

Tripp's eyebrows shot up. "He told you about her?"

I nodded, and Tripp crossed his hands over his chest as he grinned. "Damn, girl, what have you done to Kerrington?"

Well, that was what I was wondering, too. "I think he may have decided taking me there was a mistake. I . . . we . . . things got a little heated on the porch and then he stopped it and brought me back here. He said he had things to do. Just like that. No other explanation. It was weird."

Tripp frowned and sat there quietly a moment.

"You two have, uh, had sex before, right? That was my understanding."

I nodded.

"And today that didn't happen," he continued.

"No, he was really ready to get rid of me."

Tripp rubbed his chin and then shook his head. "I don't know what the hell is up. That doesn't sound like the guy I know." He leaned forward, resting his elbows on his knees. "Are you okay? Did he upset you?"

I was confused and a little hurt, but I was okay. I smiled. "I'm fine. Just not sure what happened. I keep thinking I did something wrong."

Tripp reached out and tugged on the sleeve of Woods's hoodie. "When did you get this?"

There was no way I was telling him why Woods had stuck this on me. That was too embarrassing. "Um, when he brought me here. He put it on me before sending me inside."

Tripp had a small smile tugging on his lips. "Did he see my bike?"

I nodded.

"What did he say when he put that on you?"

"Um, he told me to go inside and put on baggy clothes."

Tripp cackled with laughter and leaned back in his seat. Once he was done laughing, he took in my sweatpants and then looked back up at me. "You did as you were told."

I nodded again.

"He likes you. He may be a little freaked out and doing stupid shit, but he likes you. The baggy clothes are because he doesn't want me looking at you and getting any ideas. Ker-

147

rington has gone possessive. Never seen it before, but it is funny as hell. I think I'll text him that we're going swimming and see how fast his jealous ass gets over here."

"No, don't! He was going to deal with his dad, I think."

Tripp grinned. "I was kidding. It's just funny."

He went quiet, and I hated the awkward silence. However, I was relieved that he thought Woods was acting weird because he was feeling possessive toward me. Maybe it was wrong to want that, but it made me feel tingly and warm.

"I guess I should plan on traveling alone when I head out."

I wasn't sure yet. "That depends on when you're leaving and if Woods really is interested in something more with me. If this is just a fling for him, then I may be ready to run soon myself."

⚹

That night I woke up screaming, with Tripp holding me again. It was screwing with my sleep and his. I didn't blame him if he left soon just so he could sleep without the nightly interruptions. My eyes felt puffy from the crying I'd done this time. Sometimes the screams were mixed with sobbing. Tonight had been one of those nights, and this morning I'd spent an hour in the bathroom trying to cover up the puffiness with makeup. I wasn't sure it helped.

"Girl, I got an eight top of women who came in here requesting me or I'd take table six for you," Jimmy said with wide eyes as he walked into the kitchen.

"What's wrong with six?" I asked, tying my apron on.

"Not sure how much you know, but Woods broke it off with that uptight Greystone heiress. My guess is Daddy is pissed. Anyway, the heiress, her equally uptight mother, and

Mrs. Kerrington are sitting at six. There can be nothing good about that gathering."

Oh no. I didn't want to deal with those three. But I didn't have a choice. It was just Jimmy and me for the breakfast shift. We would have more help for the lunch shift.

"I've scared you. Shit. I'm sorry. It's okay. You didn't piss them off, Woods did. You just serve them their food and all should be good."

He was right. They didn't even know I existed. Besides, I wasn't sure what was going on with Woods. Yesterday he'd completely confused me.

"I can do it," I assured Jimmy, taking my tray of waters out to table four.

Once I had that table served and orders taken, I made my way over to table six. All three women seemed to be in deep conversation. I almost walked past them and gave them a few more moments before interrupting. But then that could have pissed them off, and I didn't want to add to this drama.

"Good morning," I said in more of a squeak than a greeting. Fantastic. Mrs. Kerrington flashed an annoyed look my way. I had never met her, but I recognized those dark brown eyes glaring at me. There was no mistaking she was Woods's mother.

"Sparkling water."

"Evian with a glass of ice," Angelina said.

"The same," the third lady, who had to be her mother, informed me without looking at me.

I quickly headed to the kitchen and took a deep breath. They were just like all the other guests. No reason to panic. I fixed their drinks and went back out to serve them.

"He just needs time. He's never been one to like being told

what to do. It's not you, darling. He's a male and he is as red-blooded as they come. The boy wants to sow his wild oats." Woods's mother was reaching across the table and patting Angelina's hand as she said this.

"I don't think that's it. He truly doesn't like me. He said that we'd be miserable together. And maybe he's right. I want things he doesn't. Obviously."

Mrs. Kerrington sighed. "Yes. Well, his father is very disappointed in him. We expected him to think about something other than himself this time. But he's a spoiled boy. He has always had his way. This is my fault of course. I should have told him no more often."

I set the waters down in front of them and tried to be as invisible as possible.

"Bring us a fruit tray, please, and make sure the kiwi is included."

I nodded once before leaving. I wanted to hear more, but then, it was best that I didn't. I wanted to argue with them. Woods wasn't selfish. He wasn't some kid having a temper tantrum. He was a grown man tired of being controlled and manipulated. And who did Angelina think she was? She wanted different things *obviously*. Like she was so noble. Bitch.

I slammed the door behind me and let out an aggravated growl.

"Whoa, sugar. You look ready to tear someone up," Jimmy said as he set an order on his tray.

"Woods's mother is infuriating. And that . . . that, ugh . . . God, I'm glad he isn't marrying that woman. She's just . . . I want to slap her."

Jimmy started to chuckle, when the door behind me closed and his eyes went wide. I was almost afraid to turn around.

"I have to agree with you on both accounts." Woods's sexy voice was amused. I turned around and took in the sight of him. His dark hair was messily styled and his jeans hugged his hips perfectly. The white oxford shirt he was wearing only made his olive complexion stand out even more.

"I'm sorry," I managed to say as my heart rate picked up. I stared at his hand and thought about how that hand felt as it slipped under my shorts yesterday.

"Don't be. I said I agreed with you." I lifted my eyes to meet his. He thought it was funny I didn't like his mother or his former fiancée. I could see it in his eyes.

"Good morning," he said, and glanced behind me toward the kitchen staff, who I knew were a more rapt audience than they let on.

"Good morning," I replied.

"I'll take out their fruit," he said, walking over to get it. I hadn't even ordered it yet.

"That can't be theirs; I haven't entered their order," I said as he made his way to the door with the fruit that included kiwi.

"It's theirs. My mother rarely orders anything else for breakfast. This crew knows that."

Then he was out the door.

"Order is up for table four," Harold called out from the fry station. I went and got their food.

I tried not to look over at the table that I knew Woods was at with Angelina. I could hear him talking, and out of the corner of my eye I could see he had sat down with them. My stomach knotted up at the thought.

I managed to get the correct orders to the customers at table four. Then it took all my willpower not to go running back to the kitchen to hide from seeing this. But although Woods had brought them their food, I was the server. I needed to make sure they didn't need anything. Especially since Woods was now sitting with them.

"Is there anything I can get for you?" I asked his mother directly. He'd taken the seat beside Angelina, and I couldn't look over at them.

"More sparkling water, but this time don't use so much ice and add a few raspberries to it." Her tone was annoyed and I wasn't sure if it was due to Woods or my service.

I nodded and headed back to the kitchen.

Jimmy stood there with his hands on his hips waiting for me.

"What the fuck was that all about?" he asked.

I wasn't sure what he was referring to. "What?" I asked, confused.

Jimmy waved his hand at the door and back to me. "The crazy shit I saw going on with you and our *boss*? Please don't tell me you're the reason Woods has gone all renegade on his parents. This will not end well," he hissed, picking up his tray.

I wasn't sure anymore how I felt. I shook my head. "I don't think so." That was the best answer I had.

"You don't 'think so'?" he asked with an incredulous look on his face. "For real, girl, if you're the reason, you'd know. Not sure what I think about all this or you, but word of caution, he's a Kerrington. Be careful."

Jimmy sauntered out of the kitchen and I watched him go. He acted as if being a Kerrington was a bad thing. Nothing about Woods was bad that I'd seen.

I fixed the sparkling water with less ice and fresh raspberries and then took it out to Woods's mother. I refused to look over at Woods.

Their talking ceased as I approached, and the silence at the table was uncomfortable. I didn't stick around. I went to take drink orders for table one, which had just been seated, and focused on helping my other customers.

When I walked back out into the dining room ten minutes later, Woods was standing up and walking out with the women. I hated that it upset me. Was this what Jimmy meant? He would never truly not be a part of them. He would eventually go back to her.

I managed to finish my shift, and once my apron was tossed into the dirty hamper, I was ready to get out of here.

"Mr. Kerrington called down and asked that you see him in his office before you leave, Della," Juan called from the back.

Oh, crap. "Thanks," I replied, and headed for Woods's office. Had I messed up with his mother? I hated this feeling. I hated wanting to please him and not ever being sure if I had. And I hated that he'd left with them. Where had he gone? Had he kissed her? Had he apologized? Was he engaged again? Was he about to tell me he had decided yesterday was a mistake? Maybe he'd been turned off by my response to him on the porch and my inability to be controlled.

I knocked on the door and waited. I hoped he wasn't here and I could get out of here before—The door swung open and Woods reached out and pulled me inside before slamming it and locking it behind him with a swift click.

Then he was on me. His hands were clenched firmly on my waist, and his mouth was hungrily nipping at my bottom lip. There was no sweetness to his tongue's invasion into my mouth.

He reached down, grabbed my leg, and hiked it up to wrap around his waist, then he cupped my butt and continued to assault my mouth with delicious flicks of his tongue.

I wrapped my arms around his neck and held on. This wasn't what I had expected, but I was so lost in the pleasure of it all I didn't care.

"Did you change out of those shorts and into baggy pants yesterday?" Woods asked as his mouth traveled down my neck.

"Yes," I replied breathlessly.

"Tripp didn't see that sweet wet spot?" His naughty words caused me to whimper and wiggle closer to him.

"No, I wore your hoodie and a pair of sweats the rest of the day," I assured him.

"Good," he growled, and wrapped his arms around my back, carried me over to his desk, and sat me down. "I need to taste it. *Now*."

Before I could figure out what he was talking about, he pushed my skirt up, grabbed my panties, and tugged hard enough that the sound of ripping fabric startled me. He pulled the torn panties away from my body and dropped them to the floor. Then he took both my feet, bent my knees, and put my feet on the edge of the desk, leaving me completely open. I was panting with anticipation as he fell to his knees and began nibbling on the apex of my thighs. I couldn't keep from squirming as I sucked in a deep breath between my teeth.

Finally, his tongue ran over my wet core and I would have shot off the desk if his hands hadn't been holding my hips down. He began to thrust his tongue in and out of me, causing me to greedily squeeze it with each entrance as if I could hold him there.

"I'd forgotten how amazing you taste," he murmured against my clit before pulling it into his mouth and sucking on it.

"Oh, God, Woods. Oh, God," I moaned.

My hips began writhing involuntarily. I couldn't control myself. His mouth moved to the inside of my thigh, and I let my head fall back in frustration. The pulse between my legs was almost painful.

"Woods, please," I begged.

He lifted his head, and the look in his hooded eyes told me he was as turned on as I was. I loved that tasting me did this to him.

"Are you gonna come in my mouth?" he asked, sticking out his tongue and running it from my opening to my swollen clit.

"I need to," I panted.

"This pretty little pussy needs to come?" he asked, taking another long, leisurely lap with his tongue. I squirmed and whimpered.

"I can't tell it no. It's too damn sweet," he said huskily as he reached up and covered my mouth with his hand before pulling my clit into his mouth and shoving two fingers into my soaking entrance. His fingers pumped into me as his tongue flicked my clit and sucked it. My scream was smothered by his hand. He didn't let up until my shaking body couldn't stand any more attention to the sensitive flesh and I pushed him back just enough to pull him up to me so I could wrap myself around him. I'd managed not to pull his hair this time, but I'd screamed and licked his hand. Had I done too much again?

"I was trying to make this all about you. I was trying to show you that you were special, but fuck, baby, I want inside you. I think I'm about to explode," Woods said against my shoulder.

What? He was trying to make me feel special? That was why he'd left me like that yesterday? I didn't think about it too much. I was ready for more. My aftershocks were slowing down. I unsnapped his jeans and jerked them down with his boxer briefs.

"Please, now. I need you inside me," I begged. I wanted that closeness.

He groaned and reached for the pocket of his jeans and pulled out a condom. His eyes met mine and he grinned. "I stuck it in there before I called you in here. This wasn't my intention, but I also knew I might not be able to stop."

I was so relieved he had one I didn't care.

He slid it down his hard length, then he opened my legs and looked down at me. I knew I was trembling.

"That's so damn pretty," he whispered, and ran his finger through the tender area. I watched him completely fascinated as he held his thick cock in his hand and pressed the tip of it into me. His breath hissed as he eased in slowly. "So tight," he panted.

I lifted my hips to take him deeper, and he slid farther in until I was completely full. I moved against him. He was being so sweet and easy with me. I wasn't used to this with him.

I decided he needed some pushing. He had decided this was what I wanted, and I wasn't sure why. I hadn't been calm and easy yet in my reactions to him. I jerked my shirt over my head and unsnapped my bra as he stilled and watched me bare my chest to him. I knew it was a weakness for him. His eyes went wide with excitement. I covered my breasts with my hands and began rolling my nipples between my fingers as he stood frozen inside me. I felt his cock jerk hard, and that only empowered me.

"You like this?" I asked, arching my back and pulling hard on my nipples.

"Oh yeah, fuck yeah," he replied before his mouth covered a nipple and his hips began pumping.

I opened my legs wider and fell back on my hands, letting my chest stick out toward him. "Harder, Woods. I need it harder," I begged, and I watched as the controlled pleasure in his eyes snapped and a wild look took its place. His hands grabbed my hips and he began to slam into me as his eyes watched each bounce of my breasts.

"This hard enough for you," he asked in a strangled whisper.

"More, harder," I replied.

He pulled out of me and jerked me off the desk, then spun me around. "Grab the desk," he ordered, and his hands pulled my hips back for a second before he was filling me up again in one hard thrust. "This hard enough for you, sweetheart?" he asked as he pounded into me from behind. I held on to the desk and threw my head back. I was so close to another orgasm, and I knew this time it would be more intense. Having him inside me always made it incredible.

A loud slap surprised me, then a stinging pain, before his hand began caressing the spot on my bottom he'd just spanked. Oh. I liked that. "Damn, this ass looks good with my handprint," he groaned.

I pressed back and he did the same to the other cheek. I moaned and squeezed the walls of my vagina, holding him tighter inside.

"Fuck, baby," he cried out in response.

"I'm gonna come," I squealed just as the ecstasy began pumping through my veins. Woods's hand reached around me and muffled my cries as his body shuddered behind me and he moaned my name over and over. His body jerked inside mine several times.

We stayed like that a few moments, until our bodies began to relax as we came down off our highs. His hand fell away from my mouth, and I felt a trail of kisses across my back. "So good. It's always mind-blowing with you, Della."

His words made my chest swell. It was the same for me, but he was one of three guys I'd slept with, so I didn't have a lot to compare this to.

He pulled out of me slowly, causing another gasp from me. Then his mouth was on my bottom. He was kissing the stinging skin he'd spanked just moments earlier. If he continued this sweetness I was going to cling to him and never let him go.

"So perfect," he said against my heated skin.

I looked over my shoulder at him on his knees kissing my ass and smiled. "I liked it. You don't have to keep kissing it."

He grinned up at me and took a swift lick. "I like seeing my hand here. You're branded."

I giggled at him and he stood up, running his hands up my body on his way. Both his hands settled on my breasts, and he held their weight. "I need to mark these as mine, too. Not sure how to do that yet," he said against my ear. I enjoyed his touch and let my head fall back on his shoulder.

"Hmmm," I replied.

"Can't spank them. Maybe I need to bite them," he said in a husky whisper, causing me to shiver.

"You like that. You want me to bite them?" He let out a sigh. "You're too sexy, Della. I'm so sucked in I can't think straight. Right now I just want to slide back inside you and stay there. You're gonna kill me, girl."

Smiling to myself, I turned around in his arms.

"You keep talking to me like that and I'm going to start begging for more," I told him.

Woods cocked one eyebrow. "You want more already?"

I nodded.

Woods let out a small curse. "I only have one condom here. It was a just-in-case one."

A knock on Woods's door stopped us from figuring out what to do now.

"Woods?" Tripp's voice called out from the other side of the door.

Woods reached for my discarded bra and began dressing me. I would have helped him but he was faster than I would have been. When he had my shirt on, he pulled my skirt down and began fixing his jeans.

"Yeah," he called out as he ran his hand through his hair and winked at me. He walked over to the door and opened it.

Tripp walked in and his eyes found me and then went back to Woods.

"I was just leaving," I said with a smile that was more forced than anything. I could see in Tripp's eyes he knew exactly what we had been doing in here.

"I'll call you later," Woods said as I passed him, and I nodded but kept my eyes on the exit.

Woods

I watched Della leave and wondered if I'd done the wrong thing letting Tripp see us like this. Her hair had been mussed, her lips swollen, and the look of satisfied female was oozing from her. I wanted Tripp to see that she was mine. That she wanted to be mine. But maybe that had been wrong. I hadn't thought of Della's reaction to this or how she would feel.

"I guess that clears up her confusion from yesterday," Tripp said after closing my door and walking inside.

What did he mean? "What confusion?"

Tripp shrugged and sank down onto one of the leather chairs across from my desk. Then he cocked an eyebrow. "You didn't do anything in this chair, did you?"

I rolled my eyes and sat down on the edge of my desk. "What did you mean by that comment? What confusion?"

"The part where you dropped her like a hot potato yesterday and left her completely confused and unsure of herself. Even so, she sat around obediently in a pair of sweats and your damn hoodie all day and even slept in it."

She had slept in my hoodie? I'd started to smile when the fact that Tripp knew what she slept in registered in my brain and I scowled instead.

"How the fuck do you know what she sleeps in?" I asked, moving to stand up.

Tripp cocked his head to the side and stared at me. He didn't even attempt to defend himself.

"Do you really know her? Or are you just fucking her? Because she's already been screwed over once since I've met her and I think you might have the power to break her."

Blood began to boil in my veins. I was going to beat the shit out of him. And who the hell had screwed her over?

"You might want to be careful what you say. I don't give a shit who you are or who the hell I'm supposed to be. And what do you mean, she's been screwed over before?" Then the memory of Jace sitting in my office saying she'd gotten mixed up with her boss came back to me. What had he said exactly?

Tripp held up both hands. "Calm down and listen to me. Damn, when did you become a hothead?"

"Tell me what happened with her old boss. The one in Dallas."

Tripp scowled. "Bastard played her. He's married and his wife is pregnant. Della didn't know because he doesn't wear a ring and he never comes in the bar. She was new and he showed up late at night and did a little flirting. Then he was picking her up and coming by more often. It's a big bar. No one asks questions. I'd seen him fuck with waitresses before, but I wasn't sure if that was what was happening with Della. Until his wife showed up. Della was furious more than she was upset. That's why I sent her here. He didn't have the power to break her. But I think you do."

Her old boss had been married. Damn. No wonder she was so careful to stay away from me when I was engaged. She'd been worried about history repeating itself. I was a dirtbag.

"I won't hurt her," I vowed. I wouldn't.

"She'd be easy to break."

I didn't like the way he kept saying that. "What do you mean?" Had he seen her have a panic attack?

"She screams at night. Every damn night she screams like someone is beating her. It's scary as motherfucking hell. She doesn't wake up, either. Nothing I do calms her down. She screams until it's over. Then she wakes up. Sometimes she doesn't. Sometimes she just lies back down and stays asleep. I just sit there in horror and watch her. I try to hold her and calm her down when she wakes up, but it never helps. She trembles and it breaks my heart. I can't make it better. All I know is she's got some fucked-up shit in her head. I don't know what and I don't know why, but it's there and it haunts her. So if you're in this for a hot fuck, then I'll gladly fight you. Because that girl ain't the kind you fuck with. She's not strong enough for that."

I was going to be sick. My stomach was wound so tightly in knots I couldn't move. She was screaming, at night. The frozen terror I'd seen her in that night at the party had been scary enough. She'd clung to me desperately. I had worried that she might deal with that alone. I hadn't known she had bad dreams. My chest hurt and my eyes burned. I hated this. I hated knowing she was tormented by something. I wanted to fix this. Fix everything for her.

I turned and headed for the door. I was going to find her. We were going to talk about this. I'd be there the next time she woke up screaming. Tripp might not be able to comfort her, but I sure as hell would. I'd make this go away. I had to. I wasn't sure I could live with her hurting like this.

"Where are you going?" Tripp asked.

"To find her," I replied.

"You really think that's the way to handle this? Do you not know her at all? Scare her and she'll run. You need to stop and think about this. If you want to help her, then good. I'm glad. She needs someone. She doesn't want me, and honestly, I don't know if I could handle this. I've got my own demons. But she does want you. She held that hoodie so tightly last night when she woke up and buried her face in it like she was trying to smell you that I was worried. I couldn't imagine you cared enough about her to deal with this craziness. She's smoking hot. I figured that was what you were in this for. But if you care about her enough to stay even though she has issues and it isn't easy. Then good. I'm relieved."

I looked back at him. "I'll be whatever she needs me to be. I can't walk away from her; I tried. I'm hooked. And now I'm about to lose my mind because I don't know how to help her. I just need to go find her and hold her the rest of the damn day. I need to know she's okay."

Tripp walked over toward me. "I don't know if she's ready for you to know. I don't think she trusts you to want her when you find out she's got problems. Major emotional problems. You need to ease into this. Don't go telling her you know and expect her to handle it. She'll be furious with me for telling you and terrified of getting hurt when you run. So she'll beat you to it. She'll run like hell. It's how she deals."

I hated this. He was right, but I hated it. "What do I do?" I asked him, needing someone to tell me. I couldn't lose her.

"I'll call you tonight when she goes to sleep. Come on over and sleep on the couch. When she starts the screaming, you'll be there. She'll see that you aren't scared and you can prove to her you're not running."

Okay. I could do that. I could wait until tonight. But I was still going to find her now. If only to hold her. I wouldn't tell her why. I just needed to make sure she was okay for my sanity.

∞

Tripp opened the door and stepped back to let me in. I'd been sitting in the parking lot when he'd called two minutes ago to tell me she was asleep. I wasn't sure how long it would take for this screaming to start up, and I didn't want Tripp to be the one holding her when she woke up this time. Never again.

"Were you already here?" he asked.

"Yeah."

"Didn't you just bring her home from work two hours ago?"

"Yeah."

Tripp chuckled and shook his head. "Did you even leave?"

"No."

He looked amused. "There's a pillow and a blanket on the couch. I'm going to bed. It's late and I need some sleep. Last night was rough."

I didn't have to ask him why. I knew what he meant by rough, and it drove me mad to think about the fact that I hadn't been here. That she'd been suffering and I had no idea.

"Thanks," I replied.

"Don't thank me. You've not been through this yet. You may hate me when it's over." He had no idea what he was saying. I had held her when she'd completely checked out and froze at the party. I'd seen the blank look in her eyes and it'd scared me, but I hadn't wanted to run then, either. I had wanted to protect her. This only made that instinct she brought out in me worse.

I lay down on the couch and stared at the ceiling. I wasn't

sure I'd be able to fall asleep. Not while knowing that at any time now she was going to be suffering. My chest was so tight from the idea of it, I kept having to take deep breaths to ease the pressure.

What had happened to her to cause this? My mind went back to that first day I saw her. She'd been so damn sexy yet adorable trying to figure out how to pump her gas. I'd thought she was just some carefree, fun distraction. I hadn't been prepared for the way she tasted, though. And the smell. God, she smelled so damn good. I had gone a little crazy that night. Every time I brought her to an orgasm I'd needed to do it again. I kept thinking about the fact that this was it, that one night and then she'd be gone. So I'd wanted more. I had never eaten that much pussy in one night in my life. But I hadn't been able to get enough of her. Then she'd finally fallen asleep from exhaustion and I'd forced myself to leave her there.

I closed my eyes as the pain sliced through me. Had she woken up screaming that night, too? And alone? Had I fucked her and left her to deal with her pain? I couldn't lie here. I sat up and buried my head in my hands. From the beginning I'd made mistakes with her. I'd assumed the wrong things. Not one time had she looked weak and breakable until that night at the club when she'd had that panic attack and completely shut down. It had been the first glimpse at what she kept so well hidden.

I couldn't stay out here any longer. I needed to watch her sleep. I needed to be there the moment she cried out. I walked over to her door and eased it open.

I waited until my eyes adjusted to the darkness before walking inside and closing the door behind me.

She was curled up on the bed in a small ball. Like she was

protecting herself. My hoodie swallowed her but she held it tightly against her just like Tripp had said. Seeing her in my sweatshirt like that had the caveman in me pounding his chest. She was mine. She knew it. I wanted to crawl in bed and hold her. If she wanted to feel me so bad she was burying her nose in my clothing, I could help her out with ease. She could smell me.

I was here for a reason. I couldn't sit down. I was restless. I stood in the corner with my arms crossed over my chest and watched her sleep. She was so peaceful right now. It was hard to believe she had trouble sleeping.

A small whimper came from her, and my head snapped to attention. I studied her face and waited. She began twisting handfuls of my sweatshirt; then a strange noise started in her throat. I was across the room instantly. Just as I sat down on the bed beside her, she let out a bloodcurdling scream and her body tossed and turned on the bed. I reached for her and she fought me. Her eyes were tightly closed, but she was crying out and fighting me with surprising strength. Each sound that ripped from her tore at me. I hated knowing she was lost in some unknown terror and I couldn't save her. I pulled her tightly against my chest and began whispering soothing words in her ear. I promised I wasn't going anywhere and begged her to come back to me. I told her she was beautiful and I would take care of her, I just needed her to open her eyes and see me. Other words poured out of me as my eyes stung and my heart raced. Her screaming continued, but she had stopped fighting me and was clawing to get closer to me. She buried her head in my shoulder and inhaled deeply, then cried out in relief. Her arms wrapped around my neck and held on to me as she climbed into my lap. The screams became small cries, and then they ceased altogether.

I felt the wetness of my tears on my face. I quickly wiped at them before she could see me and then ran my hand soothingly over her head and began whispering to her that I was here. I had her and she was okay.

"Woods?" she choked out in a sob, and continued to hold on to me just as tightly as I held her.

"Yes, baby, I got you. You're okay," I said softly against her ear.

The tension in her body eased and she melted against me with a deep sigh. "I think my dream just got better," she mumbled, and laid her head against my chest.

I sat there waiting for her to say more, but she didn't. She stayed curled up in my arms, and within seconds her deep, even breathing confirmed that she was sound asleep.

I eased back onto her bed and she kept her hold on me. I let go long enough to pull the covers over us, then wrapped her up in my arms again and let my eyes close. She was okay. She was safe.

Della

The warmth and delicious smell of Woods's hoodie was stronger than it had been when I'd fallen asleep. I snuggled closer, and the hard body and arms wrapped around me caused me to pause. I took another deep breath and realized that it wasn't Woods's hoodie I was smelling. I opened my eyes and looked up to see Woods's stubbled chin. He was in bed with me. He was also fully clothed. So was I. I thought back to last night and I was positive I'd gotten in bed by myself.

"Good morning," his sexy deep voice said, startling me. His eyes were still closed.

"Um . . . good morning," I replied, watching him. A smile tugged on his lips and he opened his eyes and moved his head so he was looking down at me.

"You feel real good in the mornings," he said, slipping his hand around my waist.

He did, too. But where did he come from?

"Uh, thank you. Um, what are doing here?" I asked.

The humor in his eyes was replaced by something else. I wondered if I had hurt his feelings. Had I forgotten something? Was I blacking out now? Oh, God . . .

"I came over last night after you went to sleep," he said.

Relief swamped me. I hadn't blacked out and forgotten something. I was okay. But why had he come back?

"Why?"

"Because I wanted to be here when you had a bad dream. I should be the one holding you, not Tripp."

Understanding slowly dawned on me and I began to pull away from him. His arms tightened around me and I couldn't move. "Don't," he said simply. "Let me finish."

I stayed still in his arms. My body was completely stiff. He had been here to see my crazy. Had he seen it? I hadn't woken up. Was he leaving me now? Did he see just how insane I was? I hated Tripp. He had told him. He'd seen us together yesterday and warned him that I was crazy.

"Tripp was worried about my intentions with you. He came to my office yesterday to talk to me about it before he caught us in there together. He wanted to see how serious I was where you were concerned. He was there to warn me off. I convinced him that I was more serious about you than I had ever been about a girl, and he told me about your bad dreams. I wanted to be here. I couldn't stand the idea of him holding you. Of you going through that and me not being here for you. Don't be mad at me, sweetheart. Please, I don't want you ever to sleep without me beside you again. I can't stand the thought of you dealing with that alone."

Tears swam in my eyes, and I buried my face in his chest and let out a small sob. His words were so sweet and honest. He'd been here. He'd seen me and he wanted to be here again. Why? Did it not scare him?

"Don't cry. I can't stand to see you cry. I just want to make you happy."

His words wrapped around my heart and I knew in that

moment I had fallen in love with Woods. It might be stupid for me to love anyone, but I did. I loved him. I couldn't tell him, though. He didn't know everything about me, and telling him I loved him was unfair. But I did. I loved him so much.

I wiped the tears from my eyes before looking at him again.

"Why do you want to stay near me? You've seen how messed up I am. Why aren't you running?"

Woods cupped my face in his hand and pressed a kiss to the tip of my nose. "Because of this. You don't understand why anyone would want you. Do you have any idea how many Angelinas I've known? They expected attention and devotion. They used their beauty to control. But you . . . you have no fucking clue how unbelievably beautiful and desirable you are. You're not calculating and selfish. And you make me want to be better."

I was completely sunk. This man had the power to destroy me. I moved over him and straddled his lap. I reached for the hem of his shirt and pulled it over his head before pulling his hoodie off me. I wanted to feel his skin against mine.

I pressed my bare chest against his and moaned from the pleasure. His chest was rising and falling hard and his hands tightened on my waist. But he didn't move. He let me do this. I pulled back enough to brush my nipples across his hard pecs as I watched our heated skin touch.

"Baby," he growled as his hands squeezed my waist.

"It feels good, doesn't it?" I asked, unable to take my eyes off our chests. I arched forward and ran my nipples over his. The swift breath he sucked in through his teeth made me smile.

"Amazing," he replied.

I loved him. I let that sink in as I ran my hands over his wide shoulders and down his arms. I wanted to kiss him everywhere. I wanted to know his body better than my own.

"Can I kiss you?" I asked, looking up at him.

"Please," he replied.

I pressed a kiss to his right nipple, and his hands came up to grab my head. He hadn't been expecting that. He'd thought I wanted a kiss on the mouth. He hadn't understood what I was asking. I continued to kiss him as I went down his body and licked each tight ripple of his stomach. When my hands found his jeans, I unsnapped them and pulled the zipper down. Then I tugged them down and Woods lifted his hips enough for me to get them over his ass. I continued to take them farther down his legs until they were lying in a heap on the floor. Smiling to myself, I began kissing my way up his muscular legs, enjoying each flinch of his body as I licked the inside of his thigh. Then I reached up and took in my hands the erection that was standing at complete attention.

"Della." Woods breathed unsteadily.

I didn't look up at him as I opened my mouth and slid him in my mouth until the head of his cock brushed the back of my throat.

"Sweet *fuck*," he cried out, and his hand tugged lightly on my hair, only making me more determined to drive him crazy.

I slowly ran my tongue over his sensitive flesh. His body was trembling beneath my touch and I loved it. I clamped my mouth over the head of his cock again and took him deep, then let him completely slide out of my mouth with a pop before filling my mouth with his hard, pulsing flesh again.

"Della, baby, come up here. I'm gonna come," he gasped.

I wanted him to come. I wanted this with him. I cupped his balls in my hands and began gently kneading and squeezing them as I sucked harder on the tip of his cock before taking it as deeply as I could until I gagged.

"Fuck, shit, oh, oh," he groaned. He liked hearing me gag.

I did it again, and his hand tightened in my hair and he threw his head back. "I'm gonna come in that pretty mouth," he warned, and I took him even deeper and let the gagging last longer this time before pulling back.

With a roar he held my head still as he shot his release into my mouth. I'd never let a guy do this before. But I loved it. I loved feeling his body tremble and hearing his words of praise. Once I had swallowed everything, I ran my tongue over the red head of his softening cock and he grabbed me and pulled me away from him with a laugh. "You're gonna kill me but it's gonna be the sweetest death any man has ever known."

I went into his arms as he wrapped me up in his embrace.

He buried his head in the curve of my neck and shoulder and let out a shaky breath. "Don't leave me, Della."

Those words meant more than he could ever know.

Woods

I wasn't going to be able to get any work done today. My mind was on figuring out how to convince Della that she was moving into my house. Today. I couldn't deal with her staying with Tripp any longer. That and the memory of my dick buried so deep down her throat that she was fucking gagging. Damn. I'd never had a blow job like that one. It had been completely different from any other one I'd experienced.

Della hadn't been worried about getting it over with or what was coming next. She had sucked me with complete abandon. I'd tried to stop her when she'd gagged the first time, but then she'd done it again and I snapped. When I came in her mouth, I was afraid I'd pushed her too far but then she tried to fucking suck me some more.

God. I was hard as a rock again. That one memory was going to keep me hard for the rest of my life. I had to find her. She worked the lunch shift and I had stayed hidden in my office. I was afraid I wouldn't be able to control myself if I felt like she was being mistreated or if someone looked at her ass.

I was heading for my truck when I saw Della standing by her car talking to Bethy, who looked like she'd just gotten off work, too. I loved Jace like a brother, but Bethy I didn't trust. She was a little too wild, and I didn't know if I liked the idea of her hanging around with Della. I wouldn't put it past her to try and fix Della up with some guy. Bethy needed to know where things stood and that Della was mine.

I walked over to them and pulled Della into my arms, causing her to squeal in surprise. She tilted her head back and smiled up at me. "Hey, you. I didn't see you at lunch."

The playful look in her eyes had my already hard cock throbbing. "I had to get some work done. I'm finished now."

"Oh," she said, not moving from my arms. I stepped closer to her and let her feel the proof of my arousal against her back.

"So, she is the reason you didn't go through with the Greystone thing," Bethy said. It wasn't a question. She was just affirming something she'd already suspected.

"Yeah, she is."

Bethy grinned and nodded. "Good. You admit it." She looked back at Della. "Well, I don't think anyone would mind if you brought the boss. Since he will be sidetracked with you and all, it should be fine. You're invited and so is he."

Della nodded, and Bethy wiggled her fingers at us in a wave before walking off.

"What was she talking about?" I asked.

Della turned around in my arms and took a step closer so my erection was brushing her stomach. Damn she was a tease. "The club staff is having a bonfire next Saturday night. It's something they do at the end of spring break season, before the summer season hits. You wanna go?"

I knew about the staff's bonfires. In the past I'd had to go bail several former employees out of jail for indecent exposure on the beach during one of these bonfires. I wasn't about to let her go without me.

"If you want to go, I'll go with you."

She frowned. "Do you think it's okay for them to know we're dating? Since you're the boss?"

I could see directly down her shirt, and her generous cleavage was distracting. "It will be fine. They need to know you're mine."

She moved against me and mischief gleamed in her eyes.

"Della, sweetheart, unless you want to get fucked in the nearest closet, you'll stop it."

Della tilted her head to the side. "I like closets."

Hell. I grabbed her hand and dragged her, giggling, to the back of the cart shed and pulled out my keys to unlock the supply closet. It was nice and cold in there because it was where we kept the beers for the cart girls.

I'd discuss moving her out of Tripp's later. Then we'd discuss both going to get tested and getting her on some form of birth control. I wanted to feel Della without any damn barriers.

⚙

The only things Della had to be moved fit into two suitcases. Tripp had told me he was leaving in a week or so and that Della would be alone again soon, but that didn't ease my mind. I'd just be sleeping there. I wasn't about to let her sleep alone again. Ever.

She finally agreed to move in with me but kept telling me I was going to regret it.

We'd both been tested yesterday and were clean. Della got a prescription for the pill, but it was recommended that we wait seven days to have unprotected sex.

Just the idea that I could slide up inside her without worry was making it hard to concentrate.

I sat outside on the porch waiting on Della to get back from

175

work. I wasn't scheduling her on night shifts anymore. I hated her not being with me. I also didn't do well sitting in the dining room watching her. Everyone pissed me off.

It was best for her and me if I just stayed away. The last thing I needed was for my dad to find out about Della and blame her for the fact that I wouldn't marry Angelina.

My phone rang, interrupting my thoughts, and I pulled it out of my pocket to see Jimmy's name on the screen. Shit. He was working tonight, too. He wouldn't have called unless something had gone wrong. I stood up, ready to go back to the club.

"Hello."

"Uh, Woods. Hey, it's Jimmy. I got a problem on my hands. It's Della."

I was running for the door at the sound of her name. "What's wrong?" I demanded as I jerked my truck door open and climbed inside.

"I don't know, man. She just freaked or something. I can't explain it. She was working and everything was okay. Then some teenage boys came in. Drew Morgan and that crew. They had a tennis tournament today. I think one of them cornered her on his way to the bathroom. I'm not sure but she isn't responding and she's in the corner back here outside the ladies' restroom. I'm guarding her but I can't get her to respond to me. She makes whimpering sounds sometimes but other than that she won't say anything."

My heart felt like it was about to beat out of my chest. "Stay there with her. Don't let anyone near her. I'll be there in less than five minutes. Just *stay* with her, Jimmy. Tell her I'm coming, okay? Tell her I'm on my way." I slung the phone across the seat and sped to the club. She was scared. I was going to beat the hell out of the kid who upset her. I should have never left her there. Pulling into the parking lot, my tires squealed, and I left the truck running as I slammed it in park and took off sprinting for the back entrance. I saw Jimmy's back as he blocked her from anyone's view. I shoved past him and bent down in front of her and scooped her up in my arms.

"It's okay, sweetheart. I've got you. You come back to me okay," I soothed her as I walked back out to the privacy of my truck with her. When I turned to push the door open with my back, I saw Jimmy standing there watching us.

"You tell no one about this," I warned.

He only nodded before I turned and took her to the truck. I sat in the passenger seat and kept her tucked up against my chest.

"Come back to me, baby. No one's going to hurt you. I have you," I reassured her, holding her close to my chest. "I shouldn't have left you and I'm sorry. But I'm here now. You're okay."

Her wide, vacant eyes blinked slowly, and then the look in them as she focused on me was one of recognition and relief. Her arms wrapped around my neck and she held on tightly.

"I'm sorry. I did it again. I'm so sorry. I'll leave. I promise." Her garbled words made no sense until she said she would leave. I tightened my hold on her.

"You won't go anywhere or I'll chase your ass down. I'm the one who is sorry. I wasn't here when you needed me. I should have been here. Tell me what happened. I won't leave you again. I swear it."

She sniffled and pressed her face against my neck. "This will happen again. It will always happen. I can't make it stop. I've tried but I can't. I shouldn't be working here. It's too nice of a place for a crazy person."

"Don't," I snapped, pulling her back to look at my face. I wanted her to see me when I said this. She needed to believe me. "You're not crazy. You're beautiful and fun. You're selfless and big-hearted. You're a hard worker and you don't expect anything from anyone, but you. Are. Not. Crazy." I grabbed her face in my hands. "I don't want to ever—and I mean *ever*—hear you call yourself that again. Do you understand me? You call yourself any of those things I said, but never crazy." I pulled her back into my arms and held her. I didn't trust myself to say anything else at the moment. My emotions were running too close to the surface.

"There was this boy. He was a couple years younger than me." She paused and took a deep breath. "He said he wanted to lock me up in a room and do things to me. It—" She stopped, and I heard her swallow hard. "It wasn't that I was scared, really. It was when he threatened to lock me up in a room. My cr . . . my fears took over. The panic set in."

She was scared of being locked up. Why? Had someone done that to her? I brushed the hair away from her face and pressed a kiss to the top of her head.

"Let's go home. Then will you tell me more? Help me understand so I can help you? Please?"

She didn't answer right away, but finally she nodded. "If you want me to," she replied.

Della

Woods would have carried me inside if I'd let him. He was hovering over me so carefully that if I didn't love him, I'd have been annoyed. He was worried about me and he deserved to understand some of this. Maybe not all of it, but he needed to know something.

"I had an older brother once. I've only seen pictures of him and my father. I don't remember them. I was too young when it all happened." I wasn't sure telling him this wasn't going to send me into another tailspin, but I had to try. He sat down beside me and put his arm around my back and pulled me against his chest. It was like he knew I needed him for this. His hand threaded with mine and he squeezed it. I was going to be okay. He was here with me.

"One day they went to run errands. I was a newborn and my mother was nursing me. We didn't go with them. They never returned. They were shot along with several other people in a local grocery store. A guy had gotten angry or something and shot ten people before he was shot and killed himself. My dad and brother had been standing in the checkout line when he walked in. They were the first two killed." That was a story I had heard many times from my mother as she explained the dangers if we went outside. I knew it well. I burrowed back into Woods's arms and kept my mind from losing focus and getting lost in my memories.

"I've got you. I'm right here," he assured me. His other hand found mine and he held it, too.

"My mother's mother was mentally ill. I never met her. She was in a special home. We had no other family. My father grew up in foster homes. Neither of them had siblings. My grandmother lost touch with reality shortly after my mother's birth. Her father didn't stick around to raise her for long. Mom was raised by her father's mother, who died when she was sixteen. She and my father met in a foster home when they were seventeen. From the pictures we had, I could see a healthy woman and good mother. My brother seemed to love her. She seemed happy. But I never knew that woman. We moved after my dad and brother were killed. She moved us from a small town in Nebraska to an even smaller one in Georgia. My earliest memories were in that house in Macon. My mother's wild eyes and screaming fits were all I knew of life. She could be so sweet at times, but other times she was frightening. She talked to my brother a lot. I didn't understand for years who she was talking to. It was just the two of us. But she saw him, I think."

I closed my eyes against the memory of my mother speaking to my dead brother as if he were there. The plate of food she would fix him, with his favorite snacks left uneaten and moldy on the table. Once it had gotten so rotten I'd been unable to go into the kitchen without getting nauseated. She would finally throw it away and fix him some more.

"Did no one see she was unwell?" Woods asked as his thumb traced circles on my hand.

"No. No one saw us at all. No one knew I existed. We didn't

180

leave the house. Ever. My mother believed there was danger outside. She was keeping us safe."

Woods sucked in a breath, and I waited for the questions. The ones I'd answered a million times since her suicide.

"Where did you get food?"

"There was a local grocery store that delivered it. She called and ordered it."

"Where did you get money?"

"My father had a very good life insurance policy. My mother sold the house in Nebraska and used her profit to buy one much smaller in a cheaper location so she could pay for it in cash."

"School?"

"I was homeschooled."

"You never left your house? *Ever?*"

This was what was so hard for people to accept. It was a foreign idea to them and it had been my reality.

"My mother suffered from a severe case of agoraphobia. Because mental illness ran in her family, it made her case so much worse. The death of my brother and father triggered it and she became desperate to protect us. To the extent of taking away my life. I knew nothing of the world until I was old enough to sneak out at night. Braden, she's my best friend and the reason I'm on this quest to experience life, lived next door. She was curious about us because she and her parents had realized we never left the house.

"The first night I sneaked out, she saw me because she had been watching my house at night when she was in bed to see if we ever left. She was convinced we were vampires and she wanted to prove it to her parents. I didn't get far. I only stood in my front yard and looked up at the moon and touched the grass. Simple things I'd always wanted to do. Braden came out and talked to me that night, still thinking I was possibly a vampire. Our friendship grew over the years, and my sneaking out changed and got more intense as I got older. Braden knew more about me than anyone. She was the only person who really knew I existed. She also knew I worried about losing my mom if anyone ever found out. So she kept my secret."

I couldn't tell him any more. I needed to stop. This was enough. The other was too dark and it hurt too much.

"Where's your mom?"

"She's dead."

He didn't reply. His arms tightened their hold on me.

"I can't talk about it anymore tonight. That's enough."

He didn't argue. He just continued to hold me. We sat there in silence for a long time until my eyes got heavy and I slowly drifted off to sleep.

Woods

There were no words. I held Della all night and she didn't wake up screaming one time. Now that I knew the horror she'd lived through, I wondered what she was dreaming that caused her to scream. I knew it had to do with her mother. There was more to that story than she'd told me, but for now that was all she wanted me to know. It was enough.

I watched her sleep peacefully beside me as the sun rose and the early morning daylight began to dance across the water. Having her in my room and in my bed was perfect. Nothing had ever been this perfect. But my chest was tight and my heart felt heavy. Della had suffered so much pain and emotional abuse, and I wasn't sure how to help her heal.

She stirred in my arms and I kissed the tip of her nose. She was mine. I would take care of her. I wanted to help her forget all this pain and darkness in her eyes. Her long lashes fluttered as her eyes opened and she looked up at me.

"Good morning," I told her as she stretched in my arms with a sleepy smile.

"I don't think I've slept that hard in a very long time," she said, then stifled a yawn.

"It's because I'm so damn comfortable," I teased.

"I agree. All this softness is comfy," she said, and grinned wickedly at me.

"Softness? I'll show you softness," I said, flipping her onto her back to press my morning hard-on against the crotch of her panties. "There's nothing soft about that."

She made a purring sound and opened her legs so that I'd fit comfortably between them. "No, nothing soft at all," she agreed, and lifted her hips to rub against me.

I could feel the wet silk of her panties through my underwear and I groaned in pleasure. She was already wet.

"I was gonna get up and make you breakfast," I said as she continued to rub her damp pussy against my cock.

"Hmmm, that's sweet. Why don't you make love to me first," she said, reaching for the bottom of my T-shirt, which I'd dressed her in last night before bringing her to bed. I'd also taken the liberty of removing her bra, because those couldn't be comfortable to sleep in. This morning, both round globes bounced freely in my face, and I forgot about the breakfast and my good intentions. Even the words "make love to me," which had startled me at first, no longer mattered. Della was in my bed and she was getting naked. She'd started shimmying out of her panties when I decided to catch up and jerked my shirt off and then pulled my boxers off and tossed them aside.

Della opened her legs and smiled naughtily up at me. "Put it in bare. You can pull out," she said, lifting her hips up to me in invitation. Pulling out wasn't always safe, but fuck me, I didn't care right now. I wanted inside her without a barrier, and the sweet nectar dribbling out of her opening was more than I could handle. I pressed her knees open and plunged in.

We both cried out in pleasure as I filled her in one swift move. The heat was so soft and tight around me. I'd never felt it like this before. I was so close to coming already that I had to hold still.

"Woods, this feels so good. You feel so good. I need you close. So close," she panted as her chest rose and fell under me.

I reached down and rubbed her clit with my finger, using the juice from her pussy to stimulate it. She began to buck under me, and I moved in and out of her slowly. Once she lost it and the walls of her heat started squeezing me, I was going to have to pull out. I was too close. The sensation was killing me.

"Just like that. Oh, Woods, yes, rub it, yes, ohmygod, yes." Her begging and cries came to a halt right before she shuddered underneath me and cried out my name.

I moved in her one more time before jerking out and coming all over her stomach. Seeing my spunk pooled up on her flat stomach only made my chest clench tighter. Mine. I'd marked her again. She was mine.

I slowly stood up and got a warm washcloth to clean her off. She was staring down at my mess and grinning when I got back. I started to wipe it off and she giggled.

"What's so funny?" I asked. I loved hearing her laugh.

"I've never had a guy come on me like that before. I think I liked it."

The idea of any other guy's come getting anywhere near her pissed me off. I didn't want a visual of Della and some other guy. How many guys could she have been with? She'd missed most of her life locked up by her mother.

"You look upset. What did I say wrong?"

I finished cleaning her off, then looked up at her. "You didn't say anything wrong. I just . . . I just don't like thinking about you and another guy."

She sat up on her elbows. "I've only been with three, counting you."

Two more than what would make me happy. But it wasn't fair to get pissed. I had slept with more girls than I could count.

"You were my second, if that helps."

Her second? What the fuck . . . did that mean? Ah, hell. I didn't want to think about this. She'd had sex after our first time together. I had with Angelina. But fuck me if it wasn't hard to swallow. She'd gone to Dallas and hooked up with her married boss there. Why had I walked away from her that night? Because she was a one-night stand. A one-night stand that completely blew my mind, but still. I'd done what we both expected me to do. Or had she?

I couldn't think about this. I shoved off the bed and stalked back to the bathroom to calm down. This was not her fault. I was becoming a complete possessive bastard and she didn't deserve that.

A small hand touched my shoulder. "Are you okay?"

I turned around and she was standing completely naked with a worried frown on her forehead. She'd woken up in a happy mood and I had ruined it with my need to own her. What was wrong with me?

I pulled her to me until her breasts brushed my chest. "I'm sorry. I'm an ass. I got all pissy thinking about someone else . . . about some . . . shit. I can't even say it."

Della stepped closer, ran her hands up my chest, and locked them behind my neck.

"No one's ever been inside me without a condom on. Only you. When this week is over, you'll be the only man to ever fill me with his come."

The caveman in me was beating his chest at the idea of

finding my release deep inside her and letting my seed coat the tight little hole I was obsessed with.

I brushed away the hair in her face and tilted her chin up until I could press my lips firmly against hers. This girl was going to consume me.

Della

The rest of the week Woods brought me to work every day and sat at an empty table while I worked. When my shift was over he asked me to tell him something I'd always wanted to do but hadn't gotten the chance. Every day he made it happen. We went boating, took a helicopter ride, went parasailing, and ate raw oysters. He rarely left my side. The sex was amazing, and it just seemed to be getting better and more intense. I wasn't having night terrors anymore, either. I slept deeply and woke up the next day relaxed and rested.

Tonight was the staff's bonfire, and I was expected to be there. I still wasn't sure taking Woods was a good idea. Other than Bethy and Jimmy, no one knew we were dating. I hadn't run into anyone else on our dates. I dressed in a bikini and put a matching sundress over it. I wasn't sure I was brave enough to swim, but Bethy said everyone at least got their feet wet. I was prepared for that and more.

Woods parked his truck and came around to get me because he was determined I shouldn't open a car door by myself. It was cute really.

His hand slipped into mine and he held it. This was it. If any staff member was curious about the two of us, Woods was about to make the situation very clear.

"Sure you don't want to turn and run?" I asked, smiling up at him.

"Nope."

"They may treat me differently," I replied, thinking it could cause some hard feelings with other workers.

"I'll fire them."

I stopped and looked up at him. He was grinning. I slapped his arm. "That wasn't funny."

"Yeah, it was. Besides, if they upset you, I will fire them."

Mental note: Don't tell him if anyone upsets me.

The smell of burning wood and the sound of music filled the air as we walked into the gathering of people. Some were dancing. Others were roasting something over the fire and a few were playing volleyball in the moonlight.

"Thirsty?" Woods asked, leading me over to the keg that was sitting up on blocks.

"I don't much like beer from a keg. I had it once and got sick," I told him.

He frowned. "How much did you drink?"

"I funneled it, actually, so I'm not sure."

Woods's eyebrows shot up. "You funneled beer?"

It had been one of the items on my checklist of things to do: Go to a party and drink lots of beer. I hadn't known about funneling, but it hadn't been hard to get me to try it. Braden had warned me I'd get sick, but I'd tried it anyway.

"Yeah. Dumb decision. Frat party," I explained. It was at that party I'd met the guy I'd given my virginity to. Three dates later he'd talked me into sex. I'd been so naive and stupid.

"You're here," Bethy said, smiling as she walked up with a large red solo cup in her hand. "Drink up. The beer's free."

I shook my head.

"Della doesn't drink beer from kegs. Anything else to drink around here?" Woods asked.

Bethy nodded and walked over to a cooler and threw me a bottle of water. Perfect.

"Thank you," I told her, and she saluted me before walking back over to the people dancing. Jace stepped out and wrapped his arms around her.

"Are you against me drinking beer from a keg?" Woods asked.

I shook my head and took a sip of my water.

"Good, I need something." He walked over there and I stayed where I was. I couldn't follow him everywhere he went. I was becoming too needy where he was concerned. I didn't want to be codependent. My psychiatrist had talked to me about that. She said I needed to work hard to be independent and that it could be difficult for me after the life I'd lived.

"Hey, Della, right?" a guy I didn't recognize said with a slight slur.

I nodded. I wasn't sure who he was or how he knew my name.

"Nelton, I'm the tennis pro at the club," he said with a wink.

I nodded and glanced over to see Harold from the kitchen talking to Woods.

"Nice to meet you," I replied.

"I've been watching you. Wasn't sure if you were available or not." He took a step closer and I managed to move to the right without looking like I was trying to get away from him.

"Oh" was all I said. I wasn't sure I needed to announce that I was in a relationship with Woods.

"You a friend of Mr. Kerrington's? I saw you show up with him."

"Can I help you, Nelton?" Woods said just before he moved

in behind me. I let out the sigh of relief. I hadn't wanted to answer that.

"No, sir. I was just getting to know Della." Woods's hand slipped over my stomach, and he left it splayed there in a possessive gesture. Nelton didn't miss it. His eyes widened and he nodded.

"Good to meet you, Della," he replied. "See ya, Mr. Kerrington." Then he sauntered away.

"I can't leave you alone for three minutes," he said before taking a small nibble on my ear.

"Your tennis pro is creepy," I told him.

Woods chuckled. "I agree, but the cougars love him. I know for a fact he sleeps with several of them, but it keeps them happy, so we don't let him go. Not good for business."

I wasn't sure what the cougars were, but I didn't ask. I needed to pee. I glanced around and saw there were no restrooms anywhere. I found Bethy and decided to go ask her. "I need to ask Bethy something. I'll be back," I said before hurrying off. I didn't want to tell him I had to pee. I preferred to just ask Bethy.

She saw me headed her way alone and stepped out of Jace's embrace and walked over to me.

"Hey, you okay?"

"Yes. I just need to pee. Where do we do that here?"

Bethy grinned and nodded out to the water, where people were splashing around and swimming in the waves.

"In the gulf?" I asked, confused.

She nodded.

Crap. I was in trouble.

I walked back over to Woods, who was watching me closely. I was going to have to tell him, as frustrating and embarrassing as it was. Maybe I could walk down the beach a ways, then pee. No one would see me get in and know what I was doing.

A girl screamed that she had to go pee and ran out to the water. That was just gross.

I stopped in front of Woods and felt my face heat up. Discussing bodily functions with guys was just not something I was good at.

"What's wrong?" he asked.

I ducked my head and took a deep breath. "I have to pee."

He didn't say anything at first and then he chuckled. "That's why you ran off to find Bethy?"

I nodded.

"Why couldn't you tell me?"

I kept my head down. "Because."

He laughed harder and threaded his fingers through mine. "Did she tell you where to go?"

I nodded again.

He pulled me over to him. "Do you want me to take you home so you can pee?"

I did. I didn't want to use the ocean. But I didn't want us to have to leave, either.

"Maybe I can go down the beach a ways and use it so no one sees me," I suggested.

"Can I come with you?" he asked.

I shook my head. No way. That was just as bad.

"Just let me take you home."

I could do this. "I'll be back in a minute," I assured him.

"I don't like the idea of you getting in the water by yourself in the dark," Woods said, tightening his hold on my hand.

"But I need to pee. I'd be getting in by myself here and moving away from everyone if I did."

Woods didn't let go of my hand. "I don't like it."

I frowned up at him. "But I gotta go," I told him.

"Then I'm taking you somewhere. Either I get to go down the beach, too, or I drive you to a restroom."

I thought about it and decided I wasn't going to be able to go out into the water and pee. I sighed in defeat. "Take me to a restroom."

He grinned. "The closest one I can get you into is the house."

"Then take me to the house."

Woods

Della had asked me to wait on her in the truck. She didn't want me to go inside with her so she could pee. I agreed to that. There was no way I was letting her go get in dark water all alone, but this I could do. However, after several minutes had passed and Della had not come back out, I decided I needed to go check on things. She'd had more than enough time to go pee.

When my foot hit the top step, I heard Angelina's familiar high-pitched voice. Shit. Her car wasn't out here. What was she doing in my house?

I jerked the door open and stalked into my living room. Della stood against the wall with her arms crossed protectively over her chest while Angelina continued to badger her with questions.

"What the fuck are you doing in my house?" I roared as I shoved past Angelina and grabbed Della so I could protect her. It was a miracle Angelina hadn't sent Della into one of her panic attacks. I ran my hand down her back to soothe her as I glared at Angelina, who was watching me closely.

"This is why? You threw away your future because of her? She works as a server at the club, Woods. What the hell are you thinking? Look at her. She's . . . she's . . . just all out there.

Nothing about her fits you. Are you fucking her as a form of rebellion?"

Della flinched in my arms, and I was real close to not caring that Angelina was a woman. I was ready to hurt her.

"Be very careful what you say. This is my house you broke into. I'll have your ass locked up until your daddy can get here and bail you out."

Della was stiff in my arms, and I slid my finger under her chin and tilted her face up so I could see her eyes. She was with me. Good.

I looked back up at Angelina. "You need to leave. Don't ever set foot back in this house. And stay away from Della. You talk to her or hurt her and you'll regret it."

Angelina hissed and slung her hair over her shoulder. "You don't threaten me, Woods Kerrington. I'm not scared of you. This . . . this farce you have going on here with her"—she pointed her long, manicured nail toward Della—"is ridiculous. I would have still married you. All you had to do was tell me you needed to get this one out of your system."

Della flinched in my arms again, and I'd had enough.

"Get. Out. Now," I roared.

"Well, I need to call someone to get me. I had my daddy drop me off here. I thought I could wait on you and talk to you. But *she* came walking in instead of you."

"You have a phone. Leave my house and call someone to come get you. I want you out of here."

Angelina spun around and her heels clacked against my hardwood floors. When the door slammed behind her, I picked Della up and carried her into my room and sat down with her on the bed.

"Look at me," I said, needing to see her face.

195

She lifted her eyes to me, and the confusion and pain I'd expected to see wasn't there. Instead she was . . . angry.

"You were going to marry that bitch? Really? What were your parents thinking? She's horrible, Woods. You're so much better than that. I can't . . ."

I covered her mouth with mine before she could say anything else. I was so damn relieved to hear anger in her voice instead of hurt, I just needed to reassure myself she was okay.

Della kissed me back with equal vigor, then pushed me away.

"I still have got to pee," she said, and stood up.

I smiled as she ran to the bathroom.

Then the fact that my father was going to know about Della hit me, and any humor that had been there was gone. He'd hate this. He'd hate her. If there was any way I could shut Angelina up, I would. I just didn't know how. She was a woman scorned. She'd been tossed for someone else and she was furious.

I reached for my iPhone and turned it off. If he called tonight, I wasn't dealing with him. I would make sure Della was nowhere near when I had this conversation with him. If he pushed me too far, I'd pack up and leave. Della had a list of places she wanted to see and we'd make sure to go see them all.

The bathroom door opened and Della walked out in a yellow bikini that barely contained her tits. Just like the one she'd had on that day at the beach, causing every man around to drool. I watched her as she walked toward me.

"Do you know what today is?" she asked. My eyes were on her chest. Her tits bounced as she walked.

"Saturday," I replied.

She reached up and untied the bikini strap and let it fall to the ground, leaving her breasts bare. Didn't look like we were going back to the bonfire.

"It's been seven days since I took the first pill," she said as she slipped her thumbs into the sides of her bikini bottoms and slowly slid them down her legs and stepped out of them.

It had been seven days. How the hell did I forget that? I jerked my shirt over my head and stood up and grabbed her, then threw her on the bed.

"Here I was worried you were going to be upset because of my crazy ex and you come walking out of the bathroom giving me a strip tease. Fuck, woman, you're every damn fantasy I've ever had."

She threw her hands over her head and grabbed the head-board.

"I want you to come inside me. Over and over again," she said, opening her legs and arching her back playfully.

I pulled my board shorts off and climbed on top of her. "The first time it is gonna be fast, because I can't wait. I need to do this. We'll go slow and easy the next time, I swear."

She licked her lips slowly. "Then fuck me hard."

I was gonna explode before I even got inside her if she kept up this naughty little temptress act.

I lifted her hips and slammed into her in one hard move.

"*Yes!* Oh, God, yes," she cried out, and I let any concern about taking care of her go. She wanted the bad boy and I was real ready to unleash him. Just the idea of coming inside her was making my balls tighten. I wouldn't be able to stop tonight. I was going to fuck her all over this house.

I slid out and back in over and over again as she writhed beneath me. She was begging and crying my name. Her nails clawed at my back and I knew her marks would be there tomorrow. It made me even more insane. I wanted her marks all over me. Just as thoroughly as I was about to mark her pussy.

Della lifted her knees and squeezed my hips with her legs. "I'm gonna come," she panted. "Oh, God. Now, I'm, ahhhh," she cried out, and her nails dug into my back as she held on to me.

I let her squeeze me until I exploded inside her. My body shook as I drove into her one last time and my seed flooded her walls. I wanted to shout in triumph, knowing this was mine. Nothing my family wanted or demanded could make me walk away from this. From her.

Della

I drank coffee while I sat out on Woods's porch and watched the waves break against the sand. I had been forbidden to go to work today. Woods said he'd have to deal with his dad, and having me there would stress him out. He was worried about me getting hurt. After the night we'd had, I was too weak to do much of anything else. So I'd agreed and stayed here.

If my working at the club was going to be an issue, I'd need to get a job somewhere else. But that wasn't an argument I wanted to deal with today. Last night's high was still with me. I'd lost count of how many orgasms I'd had, but I knew Woods had come inside me five times. Each and every time had been memorable.

I had taken my pill first thing this morning before brushing my teeth. If we were going to start having sex like this, I couldn't miss one.

I couldn't have children. That would be a horrible fate to give a kid. A mother who was destined to lose her mind at some point. No kid needed a life like I'd had. I swore I'd never do to a child what my mother did to me, but I couldn't be sure. Not if I snapped mentally. My mother hadn't been a bad person. She'd just been unwell.

I shook that fear away because I was being careful. I wouldn't get pregnant.

My phone rang and I reached for it. Braden's name flashed across the screen. I hadn't talked to her in over a week. I'd been so wrapped up in Woods, I hadn't taken time to call her.

"Good morning," I said into the phone.

"Good morning, stranger who doesn't call her best friend anymore. How are you?" she replied.

"I'm good." The meaning behind that one simple word was powerful.

Braden laughed. "Good, huh? Like how good? Like he's superhot and gives you multiple orgasms, or good like you've never had better sex, or good like you're gonna marry him and have his kids?"

I had been smiling until the last sentence. My smile vanished and my heart slammed against my chest. Marry him and have his kids . . . I could never marry him. He knew that. I'd told him I was crazy and that I could mentally snap at any minute. Did he even love me? I didn't think so. He hadn't told me. But I loved him. I loved him more than anything. And I couldn't marry him. This would have to end eventually, because I couldn't marry him. He would want kids. He didn't need a wife who would eventually lose her mind.

Oh, God. What was I doing?

"Della, you okay?" Braden asked. I could hear the worry in her voice. "Shit. Della, I didn't think before I said that. Dammit, honey, I'm sorry. I didn't mean it. Think about the guy and the hot sex. Think about everything you need to tell me. Stay focused. Stay with me." She was working hard to get me back on track. The problem was, I wasn't off track. I was very well aware of the truth. The facts. And I'd let myself forget them.

"I love him. I can't love him," I said quietly into the phone.

The door behind me opened and I turned around to see a

man I'd seen only once before. It had been at the benefit when I'd had to sing. It was Woods's father.

"Don't you say that, Della. You can love him. You deserve this. You are not your mother. You can be happy. This is what I wanted for you for so long. Does he love you, too?" Braden asked me.

I stared up at Woods's father as he walked over and took a seat facing me. Why was he here? He was supposed to be with Woods.

"I can't. I don't know," I told her, unable to look away from the hard, cold eyes in front of me.

"Yes, you can. You can have babies. They will be beautiful and special like you. Don't think you can't." I had to stop her. I could feel the darkness starting to close in. Visions of my mother and her wild eyes staring at me. The phone fell from my hand.

"Let's keep this simple," the man staring at me said with disgust in his voice. "How much money is it going to take to get you to leave and never set foot back in this town again? Name your price and it's yours."

Della, Della, let's sing a song. Della, Della, come eat with your brother. His food is getting cold. He's waiting on you. Della, did you see your brother's favorite shirt in the laundry room? He said you took it and he's very upset. He won't eat, Della. He won't eat. We have to make him eat.

Did you go outside, Della? Your brother said you did. He said you sneaked outside while I was sleeping. He sees you. He just wants to keep you safe. I didn't keep him safe, but he's help-ing me with you. Don't you want to be safe, Della? You can't go out there.

201

Della, he said he was waiting on me. He loves me, Della. You don't love me. You want to disobey me and run around at night outside in the dark. He doesn't disobey me. He wishes he had stayed with me. Now he's waiting on me. He said he'd eat his food if I came to him. Della, how do I go to him? What do I do?

"Momma! NO! Momma! NO!" *My cries don't ease the pain. The blood is everywhere. In a pool around her body. I left her and she went to him. I shouldn't have left. I shouldn't have left.*

I blinked my eyes several times. I was on the ground. I touched the warm wood underneath me and slowly eased myself up. I was lying on the porch. Confused, I glanced around and saw my phone on the lounger beside me and my cup of coffee on the table next to it.

Mr. Kerrington had been here. I'd been on the phone with Braden. Crap, Braden. I reached for my phone and saw I had several missed calls from her and two from Woods. I hadn't been out long. It was only an hour later than the last time I checked. Good.

I glanced back at the door and wondered what I was going to do about Mr. Kerrington. Had I dreamed him being here or was it real? Would he just leave me like that? Wouldn't he have called Woods? I'd started to get up when I heard the front door open, and then Woods came running into the living room and straight for me. I quickly stood up just in time for him to barrel out onto the porch and pull me into his arms.

"You're okay. You didn't answer. I called and you didn't answer. Why were you on the ground? Did it happen? Did you have a panic attack? Why? Come here." He was babbling as he sat down on the lounger I'd been sitting in earlier and held me in his lap.

He brushed my hair back out of my face and pressed a firm, hard kiss to my lips.

"You scared me to death, Della. Why didn't you answer, baby? Are you okay?"

I didn't want to tell him the truth, but then, I didn't want to lie to him, either. But I wasn't positive his father had been here, so I wasn't going to bring that up.

"I was talking to Braden and she said something that triggered a memory. She didn't mean to, it just happens sometimes. I think I blacked out. I woke up on the ground. She's called me more times than you. I need to call her back—she's probably freaking out."

Woods pulled me into his arms. "Dammit. I hate that you went through that alone. I can't stand it. Fuck," he growled as he held me tight.

He couldn't keep doing this. He was getting too upset over my issues. I was already screwed up and I was just going to get worse. It was inevitable. Could he handle that? No. I knew he couldn't. He would also want kids.

"You can't always be with me, Woods. You have to accept this will happen sometimes when you aren't around."

Woods let out a defeated sigh. "I can't do that. I don't ever want you alone when that happens. I'm going to find a cure. I'm going to find the best damn doctors out there that can help you with this. We can beat this. I promise you." He sounded so determined. I hadn't been honest with him. I hadn't explained to him that this was just the beginning of my madness.

The look in his eyes mirrored what I felt. Did that mean he loved me? Had I let him fall in love with me completely blind to whom it was he was loving?

Woods

Della talked to Braden and reassured her it wasn't her fault, then went to lie down and take a nap. She seemed off. Something wasn't right. I'd never known her to take a nap during the day. And when she told me about her episode, she didn't tell me everything. I could see something in her eyes. A hesitation.

I stood at the door to the bedroom and watched her sleep. She was curled up in a ball, which she did often.

Seeing her on the ground when I'd walked in had been like a kick to the stomach. I'd feared driving home that this was what had happened. I hadn't been sure until I'd seen her there struggling to get up. I hated the idea of it. I hated that she even had the damn things. I was getting her help. Immediately.

My father had also been conveniently missing today. I hadn't been able to track him down and deal with him. It wasn't fair that I had needed to leave Della here alone when she could have been at the club with me. I wasn't doing this to her anymore. That was probably why she'd had the damn attack anyway. She'd been thinking about me hiding her from my dad and thinking she was a problem. I should have thought of that.

A knock on the door broke into my thoughts, and I closed the bedroom door so whoever it was didn't wake up Della.

Tripp stood on the other side of the screen door with his hands tucked into the front of his jeans. I opened the door and stepped back to let him in.

"Tripp," I said in greeting.

"Came to say good-bye. It's time I left this place and found somewhere new. My dad came to see me yesterday and it didn't go well," he explained.

I understood that. Maybe leaving was my only answer. It was his.

"Where you headed?" I asked.

He shrugged. "Don't know yet. I'll know it when I find it."

I nodded and glanced down the hallway. "I'd invite you in for a drink but Della is asleep. She had a bad morning and I don't want to disturb her."

"I understand. I wanted to tell her bye, too, but I don't have to. Just tell her for me."

I didn't like him thinking he needed to tell her anything, but I nodded. I didn't need to be an ass about it. "I will."

"She sticking around then, I guess?"

"Yeah."

"And your dad is okay with this? I heard that Angelina knows now. Word kind of got out."

Shit.

"Haven't talked to my dad."

"You need to. Before he gets to her first."

He was right, of course. I needed to make sure my dad stayed the hell away from Della.

"I will."

"Is she forever for you, then? She's worth throwing it all away?"

I knew he was asking as a friend who had made a similar choice. "She's it. No one else. She's all I'm ever gonna want."

Tripp grinned. "Can't believe Woods Kerrington actually fell in love."

The word *love* surprised me, but only because I hadn't said it yet. It was foreign to me. I hadn't thought to use that word, but he was right. I was in love. I looked back at the door to the bedroom and thought about Della sleeping peacefully in there on my bed. I loved her. I loved knowing she was in there. That she was mine. That I could take care of her.

"I do love her," I said simply.

Tripp slapped me on the back. "Good. She needs it."

Then he opened the door and stepped outside. I didn't look back to see him leave or wave good-bye. I went to the bedroom door and stood there on the other side of it. I put my hands on each side of the door frame and rested my head against the door. I loved her. I loved her with a something so fierce I couldn't even name it. Whatever I needed to do to help her, I would. She'd be happy. I would spend every second of my life making her smile. I needed to find her a doctor. That was the first step, getting her help.

The doorknob turned and the door slowly opened. I dropped my hands to my sides as Della's eyes locked with mine. Her hair was mussed from sleep and she still looked tired.

"You love me?"

Hearing her say it made my heart soar. She knew.

"Yes. More than life."

Instead of throwing herself into my arms and telling me she loved me, too, she dropped her face into her hands and sobbed. I watched for a moment confused and completely mystified by her reaction. This wasn't what I had expected.

"Della?" I asked as panic started to settle in my chest.

"You can't love me. You deserve better. Not me," she cried, looking up at me. Her eyes were full of tears and several trickled down her face.

"There is no one better than you, Della."

She shook her head. "No, no, no. Don't you see? I'm not stable. Long term . . . later . . . in life I could become like my mother. You can't love me."

Her mother? She wasn't going to become her mother. Why would she even think that?

"You're it for me, baby. Just you. You're not going to be your mother. You're special and unique and we're going to get you help. But I will be right by your side the entire time. I'll never leave you. I swear it."

Della's tear-streaked face stared up at me. I reached over to wipe the tears from her cheeks and pulled her closer so I could kiss her.

"I don't want to destroy you," she whispered.

"Losing you would be the only thing that could destroy me."

She closed her eyes tightly. "But what if I lose my mind?"

I had to get her to see that I wasn't going to let that happen. She wasn't her mother, dammit.

"You won't. I won't let you."

Della sniffled and shook her head. "You can't control it."

Yes, I could. I would find a fucking way to control it.

"You are mine. Do you hear me? You are mine, Della Sloane. I will take care of you. Nothing is taking you away from me. Nothing."

Della

I spent the rest of yesterday curled up in Woods's lap while we sat on the front porch and watched the ocean. We hadn't talked much. We'd just held each other. I'd tried hard to let myself believe him and he'd reassured me with words every once in a while.

Last night I'd set my alarm because today I was on the schedule to work the breakfast shift, and I wasn't missing another day because Woods thought he needed to coddle me. I was a big girl and I could deal with things. He brought me to work and kissed me several times before leaving me so I could go get ready in the kitchen. He was behind on work in his office and he promised me he would work in there today and not hover over me.

It had taken a lot of begging, but he'd agreed. I walked into the kitchen to see a gorgeous blonde with a very pregnant stomach talking to Jimmy. He was rubbing her stomach and cooing at the baby inside. She lifted her eyes to meet mine, and a sincere smile touched her lips. I was instantly curious.

"Hello," she said, and her voice reminded me of warm honey. It was smooth and had a Southern drawl to it. I wasn't sure which part of the South it was from, though. My eye caught the large diamond on her hand. She had to be a member here. But why was she back here in the kitchen with Jimmy?

"Hello," I replied.

Jimmy glanced back at me and grinned. "Glad you're back, girl. Yesterday went to shit without you."

I returned his smile, but my interest was right back to the blonde.

"Della, this is Blaire. She's my BFF who ran off and left me for another man. One I can't blame her for because he is one hot piece of ass. Blaire, this is Della. She may or may not be boinking the boss."

"Jimmy!" we both said at the same time. I couldn't believe he'd said that. I didn't know who this Blaire was.

"Woods, right? That boss?" Blaire asked with a mischievous grin.

I liked her.

"Of course Woods. The girl has taste. She ain't gonna boink the old man."

"Would you stop saying *boink*?" I could feel my face heating up.

"Jimmy shouldn't have told me that, but since he did, can I say, Woods is a great guy. If you are in fact . . . um . . . boinking him, then you picked a good one."

I couldn't believe we were talking about this. I forced a smile. "Thanks."

The blonde beamed at me like she was truly happy to hear I might be doing it with Woods. I wondered if they were friends. I almost felt jealous until I remembered her very large stomach and very large diamond. She was taken. Very taken.

"If I don't have this baby this week, maybe we can get together and have lunch." I glanced down at her stomach and then back up at her face. It was very likely she was going to give birth any minute. She was tiny except for that basketball in her stomach.

"Okay. That sounds good," I replied.

"Della Sloane," a hard voice called, and I spun around to see a police officer standing at the entrance of the kitchen.

"Yes, sir," I replied. The last time a police officer came looking for me, it did not end well. The fear that went along with that memory kept me frozen in place. I didn't like police officers.

"You need to come with me, Miss Sloane," he said as he held the door open for me to exit. I could feel every eye in the kitchen on me. I wanted to hide from them, but I couldn't move. "Miss Sloane, if you don't come willingly, I will have to go against Mr. Kerrington's wishes and arrest you right here on the club's grounds."

Arrest me? My heart raced at the memory of handcuffs clicking around my wrists as the officer read me my rights. I had to fight this. Now was not the time to zone out. I couldn't have an attack right now. I had to keep my head.

"What are you arresting her for? I sure as hell don't believe Woods knows about this," Jimmy said angrily, stepping in front of me.

"Mr. Kerrington does know. He is the one who sent me in here to escort a Della Sloane out of the building and then arrest her once I had her in the parking lot. However, if she doesn't come willingly, I will arrest her and anyone who stands in my way."

He was going to arrest Jimmy for trying to help me. I had to go. I didn't believe Woods knew about this. Something was wrong and Woods would find me. I would not have a panic attack over this. I would not.

"It's okay, Jimmy," I said, and stepped around him and went toward the door. I didn't look back at anyone as I walked out the door and focused on getting out of the building. I was tempted to yell for Woods, but I didn't. I couldn't get my mouth to move. I was slowly freezing up.

Once I got close to the police car, the officer shoved me forward, causing me to stumble. I caught myself from falling by grabbing the front of the car. He began telling me I had the right to remain silent and I blocked him out. I tried not to think about the metal cuffs clinking shut around my wrists. If I thought too hard about it, I would lose myself.

The officer opened the door to the backseat, put his hand on my shoulder, and pushed me inside. I wanted to tell him to stop hurting me—that I would go willingly—but I couldn't. My words weren't working. I'd forgotten how to use them. The terror was starting to take over.

I wanted Woods. I was scared. Tears trickled silently down my face, and I focused on Woods. On his face this morning when he kissed me awake. I loved him. I'd never told him I loved him. I needed to tell him.

The car came to a stop in front of Woods's house. I was relieved. I wasn't going to jail. I didn't know why I was here, but the relief pushed the other thoughts away.

Two black Mercedes sedans were parked in the driveway. The driver's side door to the first one opened and out stepped Woods's father. Something was wrong. Why was he here, and why had he had me arrested?

The police officer opened my door and, when I didn't move, jerked me out of the car. I stumbled on the split-brick road and managed to catch myself before I fell and the cop holding my arm pulled it out of the socket.

"Thank you, Josiah, for helping me handle this matter delicately," Mr. Kerrington told the officer. He let go of my arm and nodded, then tossed a set of keys to Mr. Kerrington before stepping around me and getting into his car.

We stood there in silence as the cop drove off with me still in handcuffs.

"Hello again, Miss Sloane. I hope this time you can stay in your coherent state long enough for me to explain to you exactly what is about to happen," he said, taking a step toward me.

"After our last encounter, when you blacked out on me, I had your background checked. I found out that my son is throwing away his future for a woman who is mentally insane. Or at least she will be soon. It apparently runs in your family. You're already showing signs of instability. You are supposed to be seeing a psychiatrist three times a week, but you ran off without so much as a word six months ago. You have been in jail for the murder of your mother, which you were proven innocent on because your alibi checked out. However, a track record of crazy is there. I can't let the heir to the Kerrington name waste his life on someone like you. You're not good enough for my son."

He pulled out a diamond bracelet. "And to assure that you won't be setting foot back in Rosemary Beach ever again, I have evidence that you stole this bracelet from a customer. She dropped it while dining with us, and you brought it back here and had it tucked away in your suitcase. She is willing to forgive you and let it be if you leave town. The officer who brought you to me has this on record and will arrest you, and the victim of this theft will press charges if you don't leave town immediately."

He pointed to the other black Mercedes sedan sitting in the driveway. "Your bags are inside. I trust you will willingly get in this car and let it take you somewhere far from here. Doesn't matter where. Just go."

I stood there weighing my options. I didn't have my phone. I wasn't sure where it was. I'd left it in the house this morning. I still had the handcuffs on and I was very likely going to jail for a crime I'd been set up for. Where was Woods?

"If you love my son, and I believe in that unstable brain of yours that you think you do, you will leave him alone. Let him go. He doesn't need this or you. He needs someone who can give him healthy children. Someone he doesn't have to take care of. Don't you want that for him?"

I did. I wanted all of that for him. I nodded.

"Good. Then get in the car and leave, Miss Sloane."

I looked up at the house that represented the man I loved and a tear rolled down my face. This was right. It was time I left.

"Can I ask you to do one thing? Please tell him I left because it was what was best for him. Not because I didn't love him. *Because I do love him.* I want him happy and I want him to have the best in life. I know I'm not the best."

Mr. Kerrington didn't reply. He only stood there holding open the back door of the car, waiting on me to get in.

"Please, I don't want him to think I didn't love him. He doesn't deserve that," I begged.

"Woods won't care that you're gone. Stop kidding yourself, girl. You are just a distraction for him."

I knew in my heart that wasn't true, but my emotions couldn't take another hit. I was too close to shutting down. I tried to swallow past the lump in my throat. "Okay, but what about my car?" I asked as I walked over to the sedan with my hands still locked behind me.

"It will make its way back to you. But for now you're leaving it here. We need to make sure you've not stolen anything else before we release it. I'll leave the key to the cuffs with Leo, your driver. Once you are safely where you're going, he will uncuff you. It's for his safety, of course."

I didn't respond. I just crawled inside. When the door slammed closed behind me, I laid my head against the window, unable to lean back because of my cuffed hands. I watched Rosemary fade in the distance as he drove away from the small town.

"Where to, miss?" Leo asked from the front seat.

"Macon, Georgia," I replied. It was time I went home.

Woods

My mother called and said my father wanted to meet with me. I had been ready for this confrontation, so while Della was working, I went to see him. Except he wasn't home. Mom told me to have a seat, and she fixed me breakfast while we waited for him. After two hours of listening to my mother's concern for my future and telling me my grandfather's wishes, I stood up. I wasn't staying any longer. Della would get off her second shift soon, and I was going to be there when she did. I didn't have any more time to waste.

My phone buzzed for the fifth time in a row, and I glanced down to see Blaire's number on the screen. I hadn't talked to her since she left Rosemary with her fiancé, and right now wasn't the time. I had other shit to deal with. I'd call her back later. I turned my phone off and stuck it back into my pocket.

"He'll be here in just a few more minutes, honey. Just give him time. He's a busy man. Let me see if I can find him." She'd started to call him when I heard one of the two heavy front doors open and close, then the click of my father's dress shoes on the marble floor.

"He's here." She beamed. The relief on her face was obvious. She was getting tired of entertaining me. The feeling was mutual.

"Sorry I'm late. I had a matter to attend to. Issues with staff that you overlooked, but it is taken care of now. We need to discuss your future and decide what it is you want exactly with your life. I understand that Angelina isn't it. I am ready to accept that. But we need to talk."

I wasn't sure I trusted his easy acceptance of my refusal to marry Angelina. He'd been forcing it down my throat since I was ten. I glanced over at my mother, who was giving me a fake smile while twisting her hands nervously in her lap. Something was up. They must have had another future bride lined up. That was the only reason he would even have considered something else.

"Can we discuss business in my office and let your mother go relax and enjoy the rest of her day?"

I followed him down the hallway toward his office. I had exactly thirty minutes before Della got off work. I could give him twenty minutes, then I was gone. He needed to talk fast.

"Cigar?" he asked as he stopped by the humidor that Mother had given him as a wedding gift. He'd since then had a room built for his large collection of cigars, but he kept a few in here for convenience.

"No," I replied, and stood over by the window instead of sitting across the desk from him like I was a child who needed direction.

"Very well. I don't need one, either. I'll wait to enjoy one tonight. Douglas Mortimar will be here for dinner. I expect you to join us." Douglas Mortimar was one of the largest investors in the club. He had an entire hole on the golf course dedicated to him. I was never invited to meetings like this one.

"Why?" I asked, still not ready to trust him. I couldn't recall Mortimar having a daughter. If I wasn't mistaken, he had a son

216

who was much older than me and visited in the summers with his family.

"You want a bigger part in this business, and I'm giving it to you."

That wasn't the correct answer. "Get to the point. What is it you will require out of me? I know Angelina has told you about Della. I'm not stupid enough to believe she kept that piece of information to herself. She's a vindictive bitch, which is one of the reasons I didn't want to be stuck with her for the rest of my life. So, you know about Della now. Let's address that first, since it's what really spurred this meeting."

My father's jaw tightened, and I knew I'd completely messed up his carefully laid trap. This meeting had been to lure me in and show me everything I could have; then he was going to hit me with an ultimatum concerning Della. He needed to understand that nothing came before her. That if he couldn't accept her, I would walk. Kerrington Club could be left to some distant relative, or maybe even Mortimar's son, since Dad loved him so much.

"I know about your little fling. I've met her. She's not exactly what one would call mentally stable."

What did he mean he'd met her? When? How had he "met" her? I stalked across the room and put both hands flat on the desk he was sitting behind and glared down at his calculating eyes. "What does that mean?" I snarled.

My dad didn't flinch. He shot me an angry glare. "It means exactly what I said. She isn't mentally well, and you're aware of it. However, I did some research on her and it goes much deeper than I think you know or understand."

He was too calm. Something was wrong. "When did you meet her?"

"I came by your house yesterday morning. She was alone and I had barely spoken a word to her when she went completely catatonic. She didn't respond. She just sat there staring off into space. You're a smart man, son. You don't actually think there is a future with this girl?"

Yesterday. I'd come home and she'd been on the ground. Fuck. "Did you leave her there on the ground like that? You didn't think to call me?"

My father shrugged. "I wasn't going to touch her. She could snap on me the way she did on her mother. I left. And I did some research."

He had left her like that. Hate seethed through me as I stared at this man I didn't even know. He'd raised me, but I didn't know him.

"Did she tell you the police found her with her hands covered in blood? She was sitting there beside her mother's dead body rocking back and forth, completely unresponsive, with blood on her hands. The only reason she wasn't locked up was because she had an alibi. Her neighbor said she'd been out with her all night. She'd apparently been the person to call nine-one-one."

My stomach churned. Della had found her mother's dead body. *Holy shit.* She hadn't told me that. She also hadn't told me she'd been a suspect in her mother's death or how her mother had died. There was so much I didn't know.

"I didn't know she found her mother. *Shit.*" I stumbled back and sank into the chair behind me. No wonder she was messed up. She'd lived with a crazy woman, locked away from the world. Then when she'd gotten brave enough to escape when she could, she had come home to find her mother dead. Blood on her hands. Holy fuck. I had to go. I needed to hold her. She might be okay, but I wasn't. How much had she had to bear in such a short time?

"I have to go," I said, standing up and heading for the door.

"As a parent I have to make decisions that are for the best. Remember that when you think I'm controlling your life. I'm helping you become the Kerrington you were raised to be."

I didn't look back at him. I didn't care what he wanted or who he thought I should be. The image of my grandfather looking at my grandmother with so much love in his eyes came back to me. He'd said that he couldn't imagine a world without her in it. I understood that now. I wasn't my father's son. I was *his* father's son. My father's sordid, screwed-up, heartless outlook on life hadn't been something he'd inherited from his parents. They were the reason I would find happiness in life. My grandfather had taught me what to look for.

Della

By the time Leo pulled into the driveway of Braden's home, my wrists were raw and I had to pee so badly my stomach was cramping up.

"This is it," I said through my teeth, clenched tightly against the pain.

He opened the door and got out, then opened my door and I didn't wait for him to grab me and jerk me around. I was hurting too bad for that.

He didn't say anything as he unlocked the cuffs behind my back. I felt like weeping from relief when my hands fell limply at my sides.

He moved to open the trunk and set both my suitcases on the driveway. With one small nod, he got in the car and drove away. I went to pick up my bags, and stinging pain shot up both my arms. I decided my suitcases could stay out here for now.

I walked to the door and looked up at the house I had helped Braden decorate before she was married. Her husband had bought it for them four months before their wedding so that Braden could get it fixed for them to move into once they were married. It had been romantic. I had stood in her house and wished that some man would love me that much one day.

I wasn't meant to be loved like that. I couldn't be. My wanting that had been selfish. Reaching up, I pressed the doorbell and waited.

When the door opened, it wasn't Braden, who I had hoped would be here so I could throw myself into her arms and cry. Instead, it was Kent, her husband.

"Della?" he asked, his eyes going wide in surprise.

"Hello, Kent," I said in a strained voice. My bladder was begging to be set free. "Can I use your restroom?"

He stepped back and let me inside. "Uh, of course, you know where it is."

I walked past him and decided I'd take a minute to gather my emotions after I relieved myself.

Once I was finished, I stood at the mirror and stared at my swollen, red-rimmed eyes. I looked as pathetic as I felt. I washed my wrists with soap and water, then dried them. The tender skin stung, but at least they were clean now.

I walked back to the entryway to see Kent walking in with both of my suitcases. His eyes found mine, and the sympathy and concern in them only made me feel even more pathetic.

"Thank you. I'm afraid I don't have the car. I didn't get to bring it back with me. I'll find a way to get it, though."

Kent put my suitcases down and nodded toward the kitchen. "Come on. Let's get you something to drink and eat if you're hungry. I called Braden. She's on her way home from work."

I glanced at the clock. It wasn't yet three o'clock. Braden would still be at school. She was a third-grade teacher. I sat down on one of the tall bar stools that Braden and I had found at a boutique for a ridiculous amount of money. But she'd loved them and Kent never told her no.

"I know I'm not Braden. But you can talk to me if you need to," Kent said while he went about fixing me some sweet iced tea. He hadn't even asked me what I wanted. He already knew. I'd been a package deal with Braden. Kent had loved her and accepted the fact she was so dedicated to me. He had once said it was one of the reasons he loved her.

"I'd rather just say it once. I'm not sure I can tell it twice," I said as he set the glass down in front of me. I knew he understood. He'd seen me have more than one of my spells. I wasn't sure if Braden had ever given him the details. I had once thought that she wouldn't share that with anyone, but now that I knew what it felt like to love someone and want to share everything with them . . . I believed differently. I was okay with it. If she told him, it was her story, too. She had every right.

"If there is someone I need to go beat the hell out of, you just say the word."

The fact that Kent was so worried about me eased my mind. I wasn't sure where I was going to go next, but I needed a week or so before I made a life for myself again. I wasn't ready to be alone. Not yet.

The front door swung open and Braden's heels clicked down the hallway as she ran toward us. "Della!" she called out, and I stood up. Tears filled my eyes. I needed to see her.

"The kitchen, Bray," Kent replied.

Braden came barreling into the kitchen, and a sob escaped me as I saw her run straight to me. Her arms wrapped around me and I clung to her. She'd sent me on this trip to find myself, and yet I'd found so much more. I wanted to be able to express to her that this wasn't just heartbreak. I'd made memories of a lifetime that I wouldn't trade for the world. But right now I just needed her to hold me while we both cried.

222

She didn't even know why she was crying; she just held me and cried. I had missed her so much. I'd come to the right place. This was home. Even with the memories that haunted me here, this was where I belonged. Braden was my home. She was all I had.

"Why don't we get her into the living room, and you two can sit on the couch and cry all you want?" Kent said in a gentle voice.

Braden nodded, but she didn't let go of me. We managed a few more sniffles and sobs before easing back enough to look at each other.

"Are you okay?" she asked.

I nodded, then I shook my head. "I don't know. I'm lost and confused."

Braden reached down and grasped my hand. "Let's go to the living room and get comfortable."

I wasn't ready to talk right now, but they both deserved an explanation. I needed to tell them exactly what had happened in Rosemary. And maybe they could help me figure out what I was going to do with my life now. My travels were over. I needed to live my life here. Where I was sure of my surroundings and I couldn't hurt anyone else.

⚭

I began explaining how everything happened at the gas station and then how I ended up there once again because of Tripp. Then I told them about how I lost my heart to Woods and how I would do it all over again.

When I was finished, Braden was wiping at her eyes again. "I hate that man. I want to strangle him. How could he do that to you? And does Woods know?"

223

I shook my head, then paused. I wasn't sure if Woods knew now or not. Did he think I'd just left him? Did that matter?

"It doesn't matter. I can't stay with him. You know that more than anyone. What happens when I snap and I lose my sanity? I don't want Woods to love me and be left with a shell of a woman the way I was left with my mother. He has this life in front of him with so much he's worked for. I can't be who he needs. I'm trying to be who I need. I'm not what any man needs, Braden. You know that."

Woods

The lunch shift had ended ten minutes ago. I wasn't late yet. I parked the truck and headed inside. I hadn't seen Della in six hours, and that was just too damn long. I wasn't scheduling her for two shifts again. No matter how hard she begged. I shoved open the kitchen doors and everyone froze. Normally my entrance didn't get much notice. They were used to me walking in and out. Jimmy was clocking out. He glared at me and cocked his hip to the side.

"You just now showing up to worry about the lack of help we had around here? You go and arrest the best damn help I've had since Blaire worked here. Then no explanation or peep out of you."

Arrest his help? What help?

"What are you talking about?" I asked, looking around for Della. Maybe she could explain the drama queen's outburst.

"Oh, I don't know, Woods. Maybe the fact the po-po shows up and arrests sweet little Della and scares the shit outta her, then you do nothing. You let them take her and you don't worry about the fact that she's scheduled to work two shifts today."

I grabbed the first thing I could reach, which was the front of Jimmy's shirt. "What did you say about Della and the police?

225

Stop blabbering and fucking explain yourself," I roared. The blood was rushing to my head and pounding in my temples. I had known something was wrong, but nothing Jimmy had said made sense.

"The police came and took Della right after she got here this morning. You didn't know? They said Mr. Kerrington wanted her escorted out of the building before they cuffed her. She was scared, man. Really scared."

I let go of Jimmy's shirt and he stumbled backward. The selfish, controlling fucker had my Della arrested. She was scared. She was gonna need me and I wasn't there.

"FUCK!" I roared, and stormed out of the kitchen and started running. I had to find her.

"It was Josiah Burton who arrested her," Jimmy called out behind me.

I was going after Burton first. I'd gone to school with Josiah, and it wouldn't be the first time I'd beaten the shit out of him. It would, however, be the first time I got charged with assaulting an officer.

"If you hear anything, call me," I replied, and opened the door to go to the police station and the sorry-ass police in this town who could be bought.

I'd go see my father last. He wasn't going to be as easy to threaten.

⊗

I didn't check in at the front desk when I got to the station.

"You have to check in, Mr. Kerrington," Margaret Fritz called out as I stalked past her without a word.

Deputy Sheriff Josiah Burton was in his office when I walked in without knocking and slammed the door closed be-

226

hind me. I locked it just in case I needed time to kill him. I turned to glare at the man I knew had been paid off to do my father's bidding.

"You better start talking, you sorry motherfucker, or the last thing I do before they lock me up is blow your dumbass head off," I growled.

Josiah jumped up from his desk, his beady eyes going round in surprise.

"I did just what your dad had me do. I covered everything. The paperwork is done and filed; she can't come back to town. I secured it. Calm down. It's done. No reason to get so damn demanding."

He thought I knew about this. I forced down the raging need to rip his head off and stared at him, deciding exactly how to play this. I needed more information.

"What time did you arrest her?"

Josiah shook his head. "I didn't. Like your dad told me, I just cuffed her and threw her in the back of the squad car. Scared her a bit. Then took her to him."

My chest was about to explode. They had purposely scared her. My father would pay for this. Every minute she was terrified he would pay tenfold.

"Where was my father? Where did you take her?

Josiah frowned. "Your house."

He had taken her to my house.

"Is she still there?"

"No, man. I told you I did all the paperwork. She was warned not to come back or I'd arrest her, and then she was shipped off to wherever the hell he had Leo take her."

"Why can't she come back?" I asked, balling my hands into fists.

Josiah started to answer but stopped. He studied me a minute, and then his jaw went slack. "You don't know. He did this and you didn't know. Fuck me," he said, sinking back down into his chair. "Oh, man, Woods. I thought you knew. I thought she was crazy and you were scared of what she might do. I was getting rid of her for you. Your dad said she was dangerous. A mental case. I even roughed her up a bit. I didn't know. . . . Please tell me that girl is screwed in the head and what I did was good."

I closed my eyes tightly, trying not to think about the part where he said he'd roughed her up a bit. I needed to hit someone. "How did you rough her up?" I asked in a slow, even voice.

"Just jerked her around unnecessarily by the arm and put the cuffs on a little too tight."

I grabbed the front of his uniform and yanked him up out of his seat. "Even if she had been crazy, she's a woman. No woman needs to be handled like that. Ever." I took a deep breath. "She's the woman I love. The woman my sick fucker of a father doesn't want me to love." I threw him back in his chair and he rolled back and slammed into the wall. I didn't apologize or wait to see if I was going to deal with charges of my own. I jerked open his door and made my way back out to my truck, ignoring questions as I went.

Leo. I had to find fucking Leo.

⚭

Leo wasn't in town. My parents had gotten on a plane for New York City after I left their house today. His dinner with Mortimar had been a lie. He was setting me up. No one knew anything. I stood on my porch staring out at the ocean and dialed Della's phone for the hundredth time just to hear her voice mail.

"It's Della. Can't answer my phone right now, but leave me a message and I'll get back to you."

Beep.

"It's me again. You're gone. I wasn't there and you were hurt. God, baby, knowing how scared you must have been and I wasn't there. I just need to find you. Wherever you are. I need to find you, Della. Call me. Let me know you're okay."

Beep.

I dropped my phone on the table and gripped the railing in front of me. She was going to have to sleep without me tonight. Her bad dreams would come back and I wouldn't be there. Would someone be there? Was she alone?

Della

My phone was gone. I'd unpacked all my things, and my phone wasn't there. Woods couldn't call me. Maybe that was best. Telling him that I wasn't good for him hadn't worked before. His father was forcing my hand and proving to Woods the truth. I wasn't worth it.

The idea that his father had lied to Woods to make him believe I had left voluntarily or that I had actually stolen something hurt. I didn't want him to think I would do either of those things. I hadn't been able to go back to sleep after waking myself and Braden and Kent up screaming last night. I'd sat up and thought about what I needed to do next. Where I needed to go. How I should live my life. Would I ever see Woods again? It had kept me from falling back to sleep and letting another bad dream come haunt me. It was all too fresh right now.

A swift knock on the door broke into my thoughts, and Braden opened the door and stepped in carrying a cup of coffee.

"I thought you might be awake," she said, smiling and handing me the cup.

"Thank you," I said, and took the cup. After taking a sip, I looked over at Braden. "I'm sorry about last night."

Braden frowned. "You have no reason to be sorry. I'm sorry

that you have those damn dreams. I'm sorry that I can't make them go away. I'm sorry that you found someone to love and it all fell apart. I'm sorry about all the shit you've been dealt. But you have nothing to be sorry about, Della Sloane. You never have."

Having Braden had saved me. No one cared until Braden. Somehow I'd won the loyalty of this big-hearted person who I could never thank enough.

"Do you think I'll end up like my mother?" I asked, because it was my biggest fear. Especially now.

"No. I don't. I think your mother suffered a trauma while she had a newborn and that mixed with the postpartum depression she was suffering at the time. Remember that was found in her records. She had issues, and then she lost her husband and son so tragically. No one was there for her. No family. Nothing. She just had this little baby, and yes, she snapped. Most humans would in her position. If there had been family to check on her and see her spiraling out of control, then I believe she would've gotten better. That your life would have been much different. But it didn't happen that way. She was alone and she got lost. That won't happen to you. Because you have me and I won't ever leave you alone. You have family."

I wanted to believe her. I wanted there to be a reason my mother hadn't been able to come back to me. That it hadn't just been inevitable.

"What about my grandmother? She was in a mental home," I reminded her. That fact haunted me.

"Do you even know why? Have you ever researched that? You don't know why or if this is even true. Your mother told you this, and she wasn't mentally there, Della. I think you've lived believing some things that aren't true. They terrify you.

But in all honesty, Della, if you were gonna snap, sweetie, you would have when we walked in on your mother with the razor in her hand and the slits on her wrists. You didn't snap. You made it through that and you were brave enough to learn to live. You can do this, Della. You can live a happy, full life. One that your mother deserved but was cheated out of. Don't let your fears keep you from it. Please."

I wanted that. I wanted to live. For the father and brother who I never knew and for my mother, who was cheated out of a life of happiness. I wanted to live for them. And I wanted to live for me.

"Why don't you call him?"

I didn't have to ask her who "him" was. I knew who she meant. She wanted me to call Woods. I wanted a life with him. I loved him. But how could I come between him and his father? His father hated me. I would stand between him and his family. If Woods wanted me more than the life he'd been born to have, then he'd find me. I wasn't going to confuse him by calling him. He needed time to decide if losing his family to have me was worth it.

"I think I'll wait. He knows where I'm from and he knows your name. If he really wanted to find me, he could easily enough. There is a lot at stake for Woods. I'm not sure I'm worth all that."

Braden put her arm around my shoulders and rested her head against mine. "How many times do I have to tell you that you're special? Anyone who meets you and doesn't want to get to know you and be a part of your life is stupid. I saw it when I was just a kid."

I smiled. "No. You thought I was a vampire and you wanted to be my friend so I wouldn't eat you."

Braden chuckled. "Well, that, too. But I found out soon enough you weren't a bloodsucker and I still liked you."

We sat in silence for a few minutes, lost in our thoughts.

"I took off work today. Let's go shopping," Braden finally said.

"Okay. That sounds good." Anything to get me out of this house and my mind off Rosemary . . . and Woods.

Woods

I didn't sleep all night. But I figured out a few things. If Della was forced to leave without time to think about it, the only place I could think of that she would go was back to Georgia and her friend Braden. That was the only person I knew of that she was attached to.

I called Josiah at six in the morning and had him run a search for a Braden, female, around twenty years old, in Macon, Georgia. That was all I knew. Within ten minutes he had a name, phone number, and address. Braden Fredrick lived in Macon, Georgia, with her husband, Kent.

I called the number Josiah had given me and I got the voice mail twice.

I dialed Josiah again. "Get me a number for Kent Fredrick. He has to work somewhere. There has to be a work number."

"Okay. Give me a second," Josiah replied without question. I heard the tapping of keys. "Ah, here it is. He's a lawyer. Fredrick and Fredrick. It looks like his father is the other Fredrick. The number is 478-555-5515."

I wrote the number down. "Thanks," I said, and hung up to dial the new number.

"Fredrick and Fredrick, attorneys at law. How can I direct your call?"

"I need to speak with Kent Fredrick," I replied.

"Hold on just a second. I believe his line is busy. Oh, wait. It's free. Just a moment and I'll transfer you."

I waited while classical music played over the line. I couldn't stand still. I paced across my back porch. I was close.

"Kent Fredrick," a man's voice said.

"Kent. This is Woods Kerrington—"

"It's about time, Mr. Kerrington. I don't like seeing my wife upset, and when Della is upset, so is my wife."

He knew where she was. I stopped, almost afraid to hope. "Do you know where Della is?"

"Yeah, she's at our house. Arrived yesterday in a complete mess. Your father needs his ass kicked. And the jury is still out on you."

She was there. I began to move. I started walking around the porch and then broke into a run as I hit the steps and went to my truck.

"She's okay? Is she hurt?" Josiah may have gotten me this number, but if he hurt her, I wouldn't give a fuck about his having helped me out.

"Wrists are raw because they left handcuffs on her for five hours while she rode in a car. But other than that it's just her heart. She's broken. But then, Della has always been a little broken."

Della and *broken* in the same sentence made me anxious. I needed to get her. "I'm on my way. Don't let her leave."

"You coming here to get her?"

"Yes," I replied.

"Well, I'm not so sure I'm okay with you taking her anywhere near that sorry-ass father of yours. Who says he won't hurt her again? Della hasn't got any family. Braden is it for her.

And when I married Braden, I got Della, too. I knew that going in. Those two are tight. I protect what's mine."

I gripped the steering wheel. "Della is mine. Make no mistake about that. I'll be there in five hours." I hung up the phone and plugged the Fredricks' address into the GPS.

⚛

Three hours into the drive, my phone rang and my father's name lit up the screen. I thought of sending him to voice mail but changed my mind. It was time I dealt with the man. I wouldn't be bringing Della back there. I couldn't. He wasn't going to accept her and I wasn't going to live without her, so there was no future for me with Kerrington Club.

"What," I said, deciding he didn't deserve a proper greeting. I'd let him talk, then I would tell him what I'd decided.

"Where are you? I got a call from the club saying you didn't show up this morning. They're having issues with being understaffed in the dining room, and two of the carts aren't working."

"Then fix it. It's your club. I don't care what happens to the place. You made sure to turn me completely against you when you sent Della away. They hurt her, you dumbass motherfucker. And now you've lost me. I want nothing to do with you; my mother, who helped you pull this shit off; or that club. You can't control me. I won't let you. I'm walking away from it all. I have my grandfather's blood in my veins, and I can make something of myself. I don't need you. I never did." I didn't wait for his response. I pressed end and smiled at the open road in front of me. I was going to get the one person who made me want to live and build a life for us. It wouldn't be the pampered and privileged one I had been raised in, but it would be one full of love, and until Della, that was something I'd missed.

My phone started ringing again, and the area code for Macon, Georgia, appeared, but it was a new number. Not the two I had saved in my phone.

"Hello."

"Is this Woods Kerrington?" a female voice asked.

"Yes it is," I replied.

"This is Braden Fredrick. I need to ask you a few questions before I allow you to come barreling back into Della's life. I'm not as convinced as my husband that your coming here is a good thing."

I smiled at the protective tone in the woman's voice. Della had a champion and I loved this unknown woman for that reason alone. Anyone who protected my Della had my complete respect.

"Okay. Ask me whatever you need," I replied.

She paused. "Why're you coming here?"

"Because I can't live without Della. I don't want to. She's the reason I get up in the mornings."

Silence. I wondered if she was going to say more. I waited.

"Okay. Good answer. I might like you. Do you think Della is crazy or could possibly go crazy?"

"No. She's brilliant and full of life. She has issues to overcome but she is going to get better. I intend to help her and I believe that one day soon she won't deal with any of the things that torment her."

There was a relieved sigh on the other end. "Last question. Why do you love Della?"

I didn't even have to think about it. "Until Della walked into my life, I didn't understand the idea of love. I had never

237

been in love and experienced very little love in my life. But I'd seen it once. My grandparents had loved each other until the day they died. I thought it was something I could never have. Then I met Della. She got under my skin and then she began to open emotions in me I didn't know existed. There is no pretense with her. She has no idea she's beautiful, and she's completely selfless. But even if she weren't all those things, her laugh and the look in her eyes when she's truly happy is the only thing that matters in life."

A soft sniffle on the other end of the line surprised me. "Okay. Come get her. I approve."

I smiled at her small hiccup. "I'm almost there."

Della

Braden had needed to go to a meeting at her school. She hadn't mentioned it until after lunch. She ran out of here pretty quickly after she got the call reminding her. I considered taking a nap or at least trying to. I wasn't sure I would sleep well tonight, either. I hated thinking I might wake up Braden and Kent with my screaming. I glanced at the clock. It had been almost twenty-four hours since I'd arrived back here. No call from Woods. He was a smart man and if he'd wanted to check and see if I was here, he would have by now.

It hurt. I wanted him to care. I wanted him to love me enough.

The doorbell rang, and I stood frozen in the kitchen. I wasn't sure if I should answer the door. They hadn't discussed that with me. Besides, it was the middle of the day, and normally Braden and Kent were at work. Some days Kent worked from home, like he had yesterday when I arrived, but he wasn't here today. There wasn't even a car outside.

The doorbell rang again. Whoever it was wasn't giving up. I walked out into the hall and then into the foyer. I would be able to see who it was through the windows on each side of the door. I walked to the door quietly and peeked out.

Woods stood staring anxiously at the door with his hands tucked into his pockets. He was here. How was he here?

"Come on, Della, I know you're in there. Please answer the door, baby," he begged, and followed it by a knock.

He was here for me. I stood up and grabbed the door-knob. He was here. He wanted to see me. He hadn't called; he had just come after me. I started to open the door, and Woods pushed it the rest of the way as he came rushing into the house. His eyes locked on me and he grabbed me, pulling me into his arms.

"I've been going crazy," he murmured into my hair. "I couldn't sleep. I couldn't eat. I am so sorry. I'm so sorry. I swear to you I'll never forgive him. Ever." He continued to hold me and promise me things. I slipped my arms around his middle and laid my head on his chest. He was here. That was all that mattered to me.

"I love you, Della. I can't lose you. Just you, Della. That's all I need. Just you. We're gonna find a life together. A new one. Our life. One we get to create."

He was giving up his family and the club. Could I let him do that?

"I don't want you to give up everything you worked for," I said against his chest.

"I wasted my time. I can't live a life where another man controls my every move. He hurt you, Della. He scared you, baby, and I can't forget that. I can't ever get over it. He's dead to me. That life is dead to me. I just need you."

I wanted Woods.

I reached up and ran my hand through his hair and over the stubble on his face. "I missed you."

"I've been in hell since I walked into that kitchen and they told me you were gone. Never again. I swear it."

He needed to hear it all. He had come here ready to leave

240

his life behind and start a new one with me. He needed to know what it was he was getting. I hadn't been completely honest with him. He should know about my mother and how I found her. And know about my grandmother and the fact that I could possibly have inherited crazy from my mother.

"You should hear everything first. About how my mom died. And the fact that I could end up crazy, too. I can't let you make this decision without knowing everything there is to know about me. All those things I kept close and wouldn't share, I need to share with you now. Then you can decide if I'm worth it."

Woods brushed his lips over mine several times. "Baby, I'm so far gone, you could tell me anything and I'd be okay with it. But if it makes you feel better, then tell me. I want to know everything. I want you to be able to tell me everything and have faith that I'm not going anywhere."

If I was going to make this work, then I had to believe him. This was a part of me he needed to know. It was time I talked about it.

"There was a party. One that the kids at the high school were having. Braden had been planning for a week to sneak me there with her. I was going to be her cousin from Mississippi. She had it all figured out. I was excited. I'd never been around other people." I closed my eyes tightly because I knew that telling him could very likely send me into an attack. I wanted to be strong enough to tell this story, at least to Woods.

"Take your time," Woods said, holding me close to him.

"I was nervous. Mom had caught me sneaking in a lot over the past few months. Each time it ended badly. Most of the time she would spank me with a leather belt. It terrified her for me to leave. And she'd been talking to my brother more. Saying he missed her and wanted her to come to him. That scared me. I knew the only way she could go to him would be to . . . die." I stopped a moment and took a deep breath.

"We sneaked out that night without a problem. I went to my first party. I was introduced to my first encounter with sex. Not me but another couple. They were going at it in the bathroom when I went to find a toilet to use. I was mesmerized. They were clinging to each other so tightly, and I wanted that. I wanted to be that close to someone. Sex and the idea of it intrigued me after that." That was the easy part to remember. It had been the one bright spot in the evening. I hated thinking about this last part.

"We headed back home late. It was around three in the morning. I'd been on a happy high. Some guy had kissed me and I had loved it. This had been real. I had lived. . . . But then we got home. Braden never went inside with me. She always waited outside until I was safely indoors. Lights were on all over the house. We could see the one in my bedroom from the front yard. That was our first sign that something was wrong.

"My mother normally stood in the dark waiting on me with a belt when she caught me outside the house." I felt my body tremble. My breathing was getting tighter and more labored. I wasn't going to let my terror win. I was going to beat this. I gathered all the strength I could and looked up at Woods.

"Braden didn't leave when I opened the door. She followed me inside the front door and stood there. We both knew. The silence was so telling. I didn't get far. The house was small and I walked from the living room into the hallway. The blood . . . her blood." I took a deep breath. "It was seeping out onto the carpet from the bathroom door. I saw it and I knew. It was only a few steps but it felt like a mile from that spot in the hallway to the bathroom door. She was lying there so still on the tile floor. Both her wrists were slit and in the pool of blood around her was a razor. I lost myself in that moment. I began to scream and hold her hand. I was trying to bring her back. But the truth was, she'd wanted to go to my brother and . . . she had."

Woods pressed me up against his chest and held me tightly. "Oh, sweetheart. I'm so sorry. For everything. I'm so damn sorry."

I wasn't finished. I wanted to be, but I wasn't. I'd made it this far and I had to keep going. "Braden heard my screams and she came in there to me. I looked up at her and I told her my momma was gone. That's when I checked out. I don't re-member her calling nine-one-one or the paramedics arriving. I was lost in a world where my mother was alive and I couldn't reach her. Finally, when I came around, Braden was beside me, cleaning me. Wiping the blood from my hands. Then she changed me into clean clothes and stood holding my hand while I answered questions. There were so many questions. Braden refused to leave my side. When it was over, I moved next door to live with her and her parents the next couple of years. She was determined I would live with them. I could tell they were worried about it. She had kept me a secret from them all those years and they were scared of me. I didn't blame them. They never warmed up to me. I can see it in their eyes. They're waiting on me to crack. Sometimes I understand them because I'm doing the same thing. Waiting . . ."

"*Don't you say it*. Do you hear me? Don't you dare say it. You're not gonna crack. You're the strongest person I've ever met. I am in awe at the things you've been put through and the fact you can still light up a room when you walk in. When I look at you I see life. I see joy. I see my future."

I was his future. He was mine. If I had a life with Woods to look forward to, I knew I could fight whatever darkness tried to take me. Before Woods I didn't know what I was living for. In my search to find myself, I'd found so much more. I knew now why I wanted to live. I understood love. I had found it.

⚋

Woods turned down Braden's offer for us to stay. She didn't fight him on it and I was surprised. Woods made me bring both my suitcases. We didn't go far, because I wasn't ready to leave Braden just yet. Woods found a five-star hotel in Atlanta and checked us in. The moment the door closed behind him, he dropped my suitcase on the floor and stalked over and picked me up. He carried me to the king-size bed that sat in the center of the room.

"I need you to do something," Woods said as he pulled his shirt off and tossed it on the ground, then started unfastening his jeans.

"Okay," I replied, watching his hands instead of his face. I loved watching him lower his jeans and seeing him spring free.

"When I'm buried deep inside you, I need you to tell me you love me."

The vulnerable request made me realize I'd never told him. I sat up and put both my hands on his chest as he lowered himself over me.

"You know that I lo—"

"Not yet. When I'm in you. Tell me then," he said with his finger over my lips to keep me from saying it.

I pulled my shirt off and he made quick work of everything else. His hand grabbed my knee and pushed my legs apart so that he had me open to him. "I need to kiss it. I think it's missed me," he whispered, and lowered his head until he was settled between my legs.

I bucked underneath him and grabbed handfuls of his hair, crying out his name as his tongue slid up my center and then began to run circles around my swollen clit.

"See, she missed me," he whispered, grinning up at me before slipping two fingers inside, then taking laps of my juices that were freely flowing from the intense pleasure his mouth was causing.

"Yes, very much," I agreed, and held his head still when he pulled my clit into his mouth and began to suck. I was so close to an orgasm, but I wanted him inside me. "I need you inside me," I panted, pulling at him to come back up my body and fill me.

Woods slowly kissed a trail up my stomach, chest, and neck until his lips were hovering over mine. He dropped several chaste kisses on my mouth. I opened my legs so that he could fit between them. The head of his erection was brushing my heat and driving me mad.

Woods held himself over me and lowered his hips until he slowly sank inside of me. The feeling of completion overwhelmed me. Woods made me whole. He healed everything that was wrong with me. Having him this close to me was all I would ever need.

He began to move his hips in and out as his arms flexed on either side of me. I ran my hands up his arms and held on to his thick biceps so I could feel them move under my touch. Looking up, my eyes locked with his.

"I love you," I said without reservation, because no truer words had ever been spoken. Woods paused, and his throat worked as he swallowed hard. I reached up and ran my nails gently over his neck. Every part of him fascinated me.

"I love you. I'll never leave you, and I swear to you, sweetheart, that you will never be alone." His words were laced with emotion. I lifted my eyes from my focus on his neck to see unshed tears glistening in his eyes.

I pulled my legs up over his hips and wrapped them firmly around his body, then slipped my arms around his neck and brought him down closer to me. I didn't have to explain to him what I needed. He knew. I was positive at this moment he needed it, too. Our bodies moved against each other. It was as if we'd truly become one. This was a deeper connection than I'd ever known.

"Is this making love?" I asked him as my orgasm began to build.

"Every time I'm inside of you is making love, baby. *Every damn time.*"

Smiling, I kissed his shoulder and held on tight as the waves of pleasure began exploding in my body.

Woods's body tensed, then shook, before he let out a groan and filled me with his release. When his body relaxed, he rolled over and pulled me with him. He stared down at me with such devotion that it clogged my throat.

I didn't want to leave this moment. Ever. If I could always be this close to him, my life would be complete. Woods started to kiss me again when his phone rang. He frowned and glanced over at it beside us on the bed. I could see Jace's name on the screen. "It's Jace."

I looked at the time on the phone. It was one in the morning. "Why is he calling so late? Answer it."

Woods reached over me and picked it up, then pressed the answer button. "Hello?"

I watched as all emotion left his face. He didn't say anything. Jace was obviously talking, because Woods was listening, but he wasn't responding. I couldn't tell what it was about from the look on his face.

"I'm still here," Woods assured Jace, but that was all he said. Nothing more.

Then he hung up the phone a few seconds later. He sat there staring at the phone in his hand. I couldn't read his face. Something was wrong, though. He was acting strange.

"What did he want?" I asked.

Woods shook his head. "Nothing. He didn't want anything. He just needed to tell me that my dad dropped dead of a heart attack thirty minutes ago."

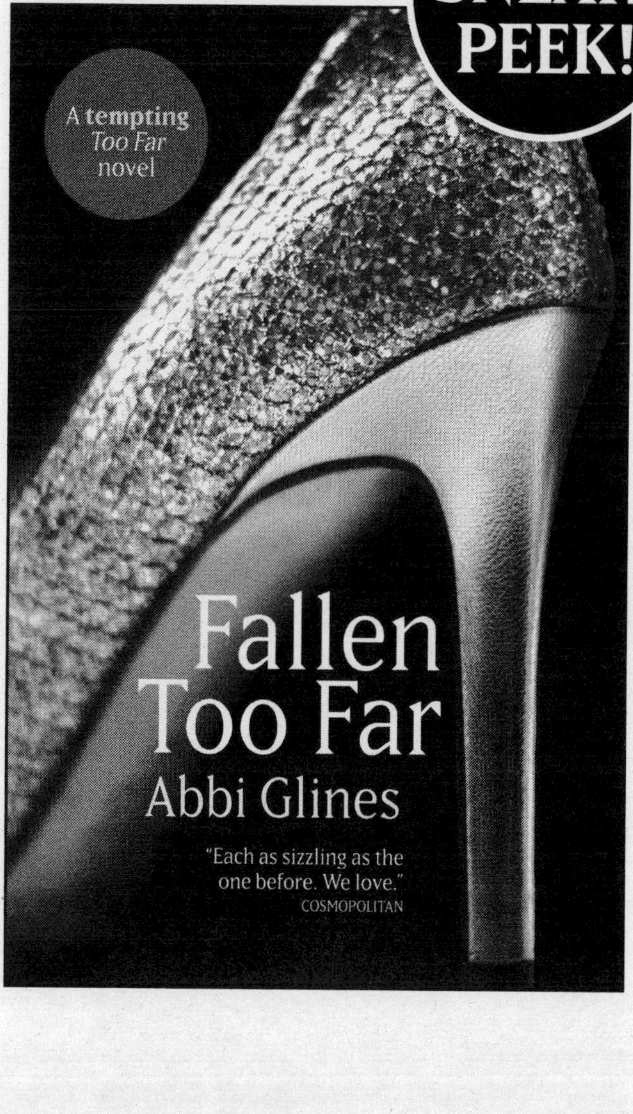
A tempting
Too Far
novel
Fallen
Too Far
Abbi Glines
"Each as sizzling as the
one before. We love."
COSMOPOLITAN

Chapter One

Trucks with mud on the tires were what I was used to seeing parked outside a house party. Expensive foreign cars weren't. This place had at least twenty of them covering up the long driveway. I pulled my mom's fifteen-year-old Ford truck over onto the sandy grass so that I wouldn't be blocking anyone in. Dad hadn't told me that he was having a party tonight. He hadn't told me much of anything.

He also hadn't shown up for my mother's funeral. If I didn't need somewhere to live, I wouldn't be here. I'd had to sell the small house that my grandmother had left us to pay off the last of Mom's medical bills. All I had left were my clothes and the truck. Calling my father, after he had failed to come even once during the three years my mother had fought cancer, had been hard. It had been necessary though; he was the only family I had left.

I stared at the massive three-story house that sat directly on the white sand in Rosemary Beach, Florida. This was my dad's new home. His new family. I wasn't going to fit in here.

My truck door was suddenly jerked open. On instinct, I reached under the seat and grabbed my 9 millimeter. I swung it up and directly at the intruder, holding it with both hands, ready to pull back on the trigger.

"Whoa . . . I was gonna tell you that you were lost but I'll tell you whatever the hell you want me to as long as you put that thing away." A guy with brown shaggy hair tucked behind his ears stood on the other side of my gun with both his hands in the air and eyes wide.

I cocked an eyebrow and held my gun steady. I still didn't know who this guy was. Jerking someone's truck door open wasn't a normal greeting for a stranger. "No, I don't think I'm lost. Is this Abraham Wynn's house?"

The guy swallowed nervously. "Uh, I can't think with that pointed in my face. You're making me very nervous, sweetheart. Could you put it down before you have an accident?"

Accident? Really? This guy was beginning to piss me off. "I don't know you. It's dark outside and I'm in a strange place, alone. So forgive me if I don't feel very safe at the moment. You can trust me when I tell you that there won't be an accident. I can handle a gun. Very well."

The guy didn't appear to believe me, and now that I was looking at him he didn't appear to be real threatening. Nevertheless, I wasn't ready to lower my gun just yet.

"Abraham?" he repeated slowly, and started to shake his head, then stopped. "Wait, Abe is Rush's new stepdad. I met him before he and Georgiana left for Paris."

Paris? Rush? What? I waited for more of an explanation, but the guy continued to stare at the gun and hold his breath. Keeping my eyes on him, I lowered my protection and made sure to put the safety back on before tucking it under my seat. Maybe with the gun put away the guy could focus and explain.

"Do you even have a license for that thing?" he asked incredulously.

I wasn't in the mood to talk about my right to bear arms. I needed answers.

"Abraham is in Paris?" I asked, needing confirmation. He knew I was coming today. We'd just talked last week after I'd sold the house.

The guy nodded slowly and his stance relaxed. "You know him?"

Not really. I had seen him all of two times since he'd walked out on my mom and me five years ago. I remembered the dad who'd come to my soccer games and grilled burgers outside for the neighborhood block parties. The dad I'd had until the day my twin sister, Valerie, was killed in a car accident. My father had been driving. He'd changed that day. The man who didn't call me and make sure I was okay while I took care of my sick mother, I didn't know him. Not at all.

"I'm his daughter Blaire."

The guy's eyes went wide, and he threw back his head and laughed. Why was this funny? I waited for him to explain, when he held out his hand. "Come on, Blaire, I have someone you need to meet. He's gonna love this."

I stared down at his hand and reached for my purse.

"Are you packing in your purse, too? Should I warn everyone not to piss you off?" The teasing lilt to his voice kept me from saying something rude.

"You opened my door without knocking. I was scared."

"Your instant reaction to being scared is to pull out a gun on someone? Damn, girl, where are you from? Most girls I know squeal or some shit like that."

Most girls he knew hadn't been forced to protect themselves for the past three years. I'd had my mother to take care of but no one to take care of me. "I'm from Alabama," I replied, ignoring his hand and stepping out of the truck myself.

The sea breeze hit my face, and the salty smell of the beach was unmistakable. I'd never seen the beach before. At least not in person. I'd seen pictures and movies. But the smell, it was exactly like I expected it to be.

"So it's true what they say about girls from Bama," he replied, and I turned my attention to him.

"What do you mean?"

His eyes scanned down my body and back up to my face. A grin stretched slowly across his face. "Tight jeans, tank tops, and a gun. Damn, I've been living in the wrong fucking state."

Rolling my eyes, I reached into the back of the truck. I had a suitcase and then several boxes that I needed to drop off at Goodwill.

"Here, let me get it." He stepped around me, then reached into the truck bed for the large piece of luggage my mom had kept tucked away in her closet for that road trip we never got to take. She always talked about how we'd drive across the country and then up the West Coast one day. Then she'd gotten sick.

Shaking off the memories, I focused on the present. "Thank you, uh . . . I don't think I got your name."

The guy pulled the suitcase out, then turned back to me.

"What? You forgot to ask when you had the nine millimeter pointed at my face?" he replied.

I sighed. Okay, maybe I'd gone a little overboard with the gun, but he'd scared me.

"I'm Grant, a, uh, friend of Rush's."

"Rush?" There was that name again. Who was Rush?

Grant's grin grew big once again. "You don't know who Rush is?" He was extremely amused. "I'm so fucking glad I came tonight."

He nodded his head toward the house. "Come on. I'll introduce you."

I walked beside him as he led me to the house. The music inside got louder as we got closer. If my dad wasn't here, then who was? I knew Georgiana was his new wife, but that was all I knew. Was this a party her kids were having? How old were they? She did have kids, didn't she? I couldn't remember. Dad had been vague. He'd said I'd like my new family but he hadn't said who that family was exactly.

"So, does Rush live here?" I asked.

"Yeah, he does, at least in the summer. He moves to his other houses according to the season."

"His other houses?"

Grant chuckled. "You don't know anything about this family your dad has married into, do you, Blaire?"

He had no idea. I shook my head.

"Quick mini-lesson then, before we walk inside the madness," he replied, stopping at the top of the stairs leading to the front door and looking at me. "Rush Finlay is your stepbrother. He's the only child of the famous drummer for Slacker Demon, Dean Finlay. His parents never married. His mother, Georgiana, was a groupie back in the day. This is his house. His mother gets to live here because he allows it." He stopped and looked back at the door as it swung open. "These are all his friends."

A tall, willowy strawberry blonde wearing a short royal-blue dress and a pair of heels that I'd break my neck in if I tried to wear them stood there staring at me. I didn't miss the distaste in her scowl. I didn't know much about people like this, but I did know that my department store clothing wasn't something she approved of. Either that or I had a bug crawling on me.

"Well, hello, Nannette," Grant said in an annoyed tone.

"Who is she?" the girl asked, shifting her gaze to Grant.

"A friend. Wipe the snarl off your face, Nan, it isn't an attractive look for you," he replied, reaching over to grab my hand and pulling me into the house behind him.

The room wasn't as full as I'd assumed. As we walked past the large, open foyer, an arched doorway led into what I assumed was a living room. Even so, it was bigger than my entire house, or what had been my house. Two glass doors were standing open with a breathtaking view of the ocean. I wanted to see that up close.

"This way," Grant instructed as he made his way over to a . . . bar? Really? There was a bar in the house?

I glanced over the people we passed by. They all paused for a moment and gave me a quick once-over. I stood out big-time.

"Rush, meet Blaire. I believe she might belong to you. I found her outside looking a little lost," Grant said, and I swung my gaze from the curious people to see who this Rush was.

Oh.

Oh. My.

"Is that so?" Rush replied in a lazy drawl, and leaned forward from his relaxed position on the white sofa with a beer in his hand. "She's cute but she's young. Can't say she's mine."

"Oh, she's yours all right. Seeing as her daddy has run off to Paris with your momma for the next few weeks. I'd say this one now belongs to you. I'd gladly offer her a room at my place if you want. That is, if she promises to leave her deadly weapon in the truck."

Rush narrowed his eyes and studied me closely. They were an odd color. Stunningly unusual. They weren't brown. They weren't hazel. They were a warm color with some silver laced through them. I'd never seen anything like them. Could they be contacts?

"That doesn't make her mine," he finally replied, and leaned back on the sofa where he'd been reclining when we walked up.

Grant cleared his throat. "You're kidding, right?"

Rush didn't reply. Instead he took a drink from the long-neck in his hand. His gaze had shifted to Grant's, and I could see the warning there. I was going to be asked to leave. This wasn't good. I had exactly twenty dollars in my purse and I was almost out of gas. I'd already sold anything of value that I possessed. When I'd called my father I had explained that I just needed somewhere to stay until I could get a job and make enough money to go find a place of my own. He had quickly agreed and given me this address, telling me he would love for me to come stay with him.

Rush's attention was back on me. He was waiting on me to make a move. What did he expect me to say? A smirk touched his lips and he winked at me.

"I got a house full of guests tonight and my bed's already full." He shifted his eyes to Grant. "I think it's best if we let her go find a hotel until I can get in touch with her *daddy*."

The disgust on his tongue as he said the word *daddy* hadn't gone unnoticed. He didn't like my father. I couldn't blame him really. This wasn't Rush's fault. My dad had sent me here. I'd wasted most of my money on gas and food driving here. Why had I trusted that man?

I reached over and grabbed the handle on the suitcase Grant was still holding. "He's right. I should go. This was a very bad idea," I explained without looking at him. I tugged hard on the suitcase and he let go somewhat reluctantly. Tears stung my eyes as the realization that I was about to be home-less sank in. I couldn't look at either of them.

Turning, I headed for the door, keeping my eyes downcast. I heard Grant arguing with Rush but I blocked it out. I didn't want to hear what that beautiful man said about me. He didn't like me. That much was obvious. My dad was not a welcome member of the family apparently.

"Leaving so soon?" a voice that reminded me of smooth syrup asked. I glanced up to see the delighted smile on the face of the girl who had opened the door earlier. She didn't want me here, either. Was I that revolting to these people? I quickly dropped my eyes back to the floor and opened the door. I had too much pride for that mean bitch to see me cry.

Once I was safely outside, I let out a sob and headed to my truck. If I hadn't been carrying my suitcase I'd have run. I needed the comfort of it. I belonged inside my truck, not in this ridiculous house with these uppity people. I missed home. I missed my mom. Another sob broke free, and I closed the door to my truck, locking it behind me.

About the Author

ABBI GLINES is the author of *Fallen Too Far* and *Never Too Far*, in addition to the young adult Sea Breeze and Vincent Boys series. A devoted book lover, Abbi lives with her family in Alabama. She maintains a Twitter addiction at @AbbiGlines and can also be found on Facebook and at AbbiGlines.com.